AN UNMOURNED MAN
Lady C. Investigates

Book One

Issy Brooke

dy. For now," she added darkly, her fine
iefly lowering. She stared at the now-soiled
th distaste, and tried to fold it up small, but
tucking it back into her sleeve. She held it
n thumb and forefinger. "Are you *quite* set
his morning? My lady?"

. Do not think me unkind, Ruby. At your
socialising and drinking all the night long
ll attend a pre-hunt breakfast the next
imes I had not slept at all yet I could be as
." Cordelia paused. She was a robust sort
ashionably sturdy, who had never been
rt of plant. An oak tree, perhaps. "I always
air did me more good than anything else.
ift the weariness of a long night's dancing."

actly dancing," Ruby muttered. She patted
d the stained handkerchief into the long
her dark blue bonnet from where it had
d her short white gloves back on. She
and looked down the road to where the
ases of the town could be seen. "I'm ready,
oke with more resignation than deference,

CHAPTER ONE

1845. England.
Somewhere in a flat Cambridgeshire field.

Cordelia, Lady Cornbrook – the dowager wife of a deceased knight – turned away to hide the inappropriate smile on her face. She supposed that she ought to offer a reassuring comment to the young lady's maid. Ruby was in a rather fragile state. She was holding back her retches as politely as she could, her curvaceous frame shaking, but it was a plain fact that no one could carry a hangover with any kind of grace.

"What age are you? Twenty, twenty-one?" Cordelia said, musingly, as she gazed over the unfamiliar parched fields. "You must have an exceedingly feeble liver, girl. You must try Mr Peeble's Salts; I used them all the time at your age. They have a remarkably curative effect. If you can tolerate the stinging sensation, that is."

Cordelia's advice didn't spark an outpouring of

gratitude from the maid. Cordelia turned to see the well-dressed girl bending double, her hands on her knees. Ruby thrust her head into a patch of cow parsley by the side of the unpaved road, and began to make indecorous noises as an outpouring of another sort occurred.

Cordelia moved a few paces back, and looked into the clear and cloudless sky, carefully allowing Ruby the dignity of throwing up alone. It seemed the thing to do, though such exact circumstances had never been explicitly covered at her European finishing school. *When in doubt, use discretion,* Cordelia reminded herself. *I learned that quite well during my short marriage.*

There was a stifled sob.

Poor girl. Though her illness is of her own making. I should give her a moment to recover. Cordelia discretely looked around to study the strange, dull landscape. It was mostly flat and utterly tedious. They were on a dusty road that was quite wide enough for two carriages though it didn't lead anywhere important, other than Hugo Hawke's fine country estate, Wallerton Manor. Here, the road terminated abruptly, as if marking that to arrive at the caddish gentleman's abode was the pinnacle of an achievement –

which it was, as a
the ironed-out fie
August in Cambri
side of the road
escape the heat of
claustrophobia o
Cordelia had taker
after dawn. This r
small town that la
and hearty as Cor
and way past the
more effort than
London park.

For Ruby,
operating on a s
torture, and walk
the goodwife was
her tender stoma
Hence the u
"Are you qu
straightened up
handkerchief she

"Yes, my l
auburn brows b
handkerchief w
decided against
carefully betwee
upon the town

"Absolutel
age I, too, was
and I could st
morning. Some
fresh as a flowe
of woman, un
likened to any so
found the fresh
It would soon sh
"I wasn't e
her hair, dropp
grass, retrieved
fallen, and pull
straightened up
first scattered ho
my lady." She sp

a sigh at the edge of her words.

Cordelia strode on vigorously and Ruby lagged a half-pace behind, close enough to be annoying to Cordelia that she wasn't walking alongside but nor was she trailing at a suitably respectful distance.

Neither here nor there; that summed Ruby up completely.

Ruby had only been in Cordelia's service for four months, and this was the first significant trip away they had embarked upon. While they had been at home, Ruby had faded into the background, becoming one of the many staff that kept the pointlessly large house running. She had been a well-bred upper housemaid who made a good impression on her house steward, Neville Fry.

Oh, the house. Cordelia's home for the past six years had been a draughty mansion near London, called Clarfields. And for five of those years, she had ruled it alone as a widow. Now, that blissful interlude was going to have to end. She had ignored the impending change stubbornly but it was no use; something had to be done.

Because she had not inherited the house. Of course, she received jewellery and clothing and money and stocks and bonds, like most women did, and she had learned to make the most of her investments. But her husband had struck at her even in death by making his estates over in trust to Hugo Hawke, and simply allowing her a few years' grace before she re-entered the marriage market.

Hugo had invited her to his manor to "discuss the delicate matter" and she had accepted. It was time to accept some of the many invitations that had built up since she had been officially out of mourning, and she may as well start with the man who held her whole future in his large, firm hands.

She liked Hugo. But she was not sure she trusted him. But then, after Maxwell, why would she?

She returned to the present. The visit had seemed like an ideal opportunity to get to know her new maid better, and her usual lady's maid was due some time off. Ruby had therefore been promoted. Possibly – it was transpiring – beyond her capabilities.

Cordelia had quickly learned that Ruby's chequered employment history was probably not due to the currently changing status of domestic staff. With increased opportunities for folk in factories and mills, household staff

CHAPTER ONE

1845. England.
Somewhere in a flat Cambridgeshire field.

Cordelia, Lady Cornbrook – the dowager wife of a deceased knight – turned away to hide the inappropriate smile on her face. She supposed that she ought to offer a reassuring comment to the young lady's maid. Ruby was in a rather fragile state. She was holding back her retches as politely as she could, her curvaceous frame shaking, but it was a plain fact that no one could carry a hangover with any kind of grace.

"What age are you? Twenty, twenty-one?" Cordelia said, musingly, as she gazed over the unfamiliar parched fields. "You must have an exceedingly feeble liver, girl. You must try Mr Peeble's Salts; I used them all the time at your age. They have a remarkably curative effect. If you can tolerate the stinging sensation, that is."

Cordelia's advice didn't spark an outpouring of

gratitude from the maid. Cordelia turned to see the well-dressed girl bending double, her hands on her knees. Ruby thrust her head into a patch of cow parsley by the side of the unpaved road, and began to make indecorous noises as an outpouring of another sort occurred.

Cordelia moved a few paces back, and looked into the clear and cloudless sky, carefully allowing Ruby the dignity of throwing up alone. It seemed the thing to do, though such exact circumstances had never been explicitly covered at her European finishing school. *When in doubt, use discretion*, Cordelia reminded herself. *I learned that quite well during my short marriage.*

There was a stifled sob.

Poor girl. Though her illness is of her own making. I should give her a moment to recover. Cordelia discretely looked around to study the strange, dull landscape. It was mostly flat and utterly tedious. They were on a dusty road that was quite wide enough for two carriages though it didn't lead anywhere important, other than Hugo Hawke's fine country estate, Wallerton Manor. Here, the road terminated abruptly, as if marking that to arrive at the caddish gentleman's abode was the pinnacle of an achievement –

which it was, as a break to the unremitting monotony of the ironed-out fields. There had been so little rain this August in Cambridgeshire that the fields of crops to either side of the road were yellow and wilting. In an effort to escape the heat of the day – and to escape the stultifying claustrophobia of being someone else's houseguest – Cordelia had taken to walking in the area only a few hours after dawn. This morning, she had determined to visit the small town that lay two miles away. For a woman as hale and hearty as Cordelia, though she was in her mid-thirties and way past the prime of her womanhood, it was still no more effort than a mere stroll around a boating lake in a London park.

For Ruby, who was fifteen years her junior and operating on a severe sleep deficit, the expedition was torture, and walking past the window of a cottage where the goodwife was frying bacon had been the final straw for her tender stomach.

Hence the unloading thereof.

"Are you quite done, girl?" Cordelia asked as Ruby straightened up and wiped her mouth with a lace-edged handkerchief she plucked from her sleeve.

"Yes, my lady. For now," she added darkly, her fine auburn brows briefly lowering. She stared at the now-soiled handkerchief with distaste, and tried to fold it up small, but decided against tucking it back into her sleeve. She held it carefully between thumb and forefinger. "Are you *quite* set upon the town this morning? My lady?"

"Absolutely. Do not think me unkind, Ruby. At your age I, too, was socialising and drinking all the night long and I could still attend a pre-hunt breakfast the next morning. Sometimes I had not slept at all yet I could be as fresh as a flower." Cordelia paused. She was a robust sort of woman, unfashionably sturdy, who had never been likened to any sort of plant. An oak tree, perhaps. "I always found the fresh air did me more good than anything else. It would soon shift the weariness of a long night's dancing."

"I wasn't *exactly* dancing," Ruby muttered. She patted her hair, dropped the stained handkerchief into the long grass, retrieved her dark blue bonnet from where it had fallen, and pulled her short white gloves back on. She straightened up and looked down the road to where the first scattered houses of the town could be seen. "I'm ready, my lady." She spoke with more resignation than deference, a sigh at the edge of her words.

Cordelia strode on vigorously and Ruby lagged a half-pace behind, close enough to be annoying to Cordelia that she wasn't walking alongside but nor was she trailing at a suitably respectful distance.

Neither here nor there; that summed Ruby up completely.

Ruby had only been in Cordelia's service for four months, and this was the first significant trip away they had embarked upon. While they had been at home, Ruby had faded into the background, becoming one of the many staff that kept the pointlessly large house running. She had been a well-bred upper housemaid who made a good impression on her house steward, Neville Fry.

Oh, the house. Cordelia's home for the past six years had been a draughty mansion near London, called Clarfields. And for five of those years, she had ruled it alone as a widow. Now, that blissful interlude was going to have to end. She had ignored the impending change stubbornly but it was no use; something had to be done.

Because she had not inherited the house. Of course, she received jewellery and clothing and money and stocks and bonds, like most women did, and she had learned to make the most of her investments. But her husband had struck at her even in death by making his estates over in trust to Hugo Hawke, and simply allowing her a few years' grace before she re-entered the marriage market.

Hugo had invited her to his manor to "discuss the delicate matter" and she had accepted. It was time to accept some of the many invitations that had built up since she had been officially out of mourning, and she may as well start with the man who held her whole future in his large, firm hands.

She liked Hugo. But she was not sure she trusted him. But then, after Maxwell, why would she?

She returned to the present. The visit had seemed like an ideal opportunity to get to know her new maid better, and her usual lady's maid was due some time off. Ruby had therefore been promoted. Possibly – it was transpiring – beyond her capabilities.

Cordelia had quickly learned that Ruby's chequered employment history was probably not due to the currently changing status of domestic staff. With increased opportunities for folk in factories and mills, household staff could pick and choose the best positions, and it was getting harder to convince good servants to stay in service. In Ruby's case, however, Cordelia realised that she was probably working her way through her previous Master or Mistress's wine cellars – and male staff – with equal enthusiasm and alacrity.

But Cordelia decided that Ruby was trainable. She was quick and smart and just hard-working enough to not be called lazy. On they went, the silence broken only by distant birdsong and Ruby's frequent heavy sighs. Cordelia had to admit to herself that her claim she was being "kind" to the maid by making her walk was not entirely true.

The young woman needs to learn either temperance, or cunning self-management, she thought. *I had learned to disguise a hangover by the age of nineteen. All one needs is Mr Peeble's Salts, much strong coffee, a well-constructed and supportive set of undergarments, decent face powder in a variety of shades, and in the worst of cases when one must absolutely appear untouched, a few coca leaves. The effect of a moment's chewing is a thing of wonder. Truly, nature provides marvels. I hear it is recommended when one climbs mountains. Shall I ever climb a mountain?*

She shoved her daydreams aside. She didn't have the

right shoes for that climate. "Come along, now, girl. Don't dawdle," Cordelia said as they drew nearer to the outskirts of the red-brick country town. It was a change to look upon houses that did not have a thick smog hanging over them.

"My lady," Ruby muttered in a tone that left much doubt as to the meaning. *Yes my lady* or *no my lady* was equally likely.

The road had begun to sprout junctions and side roads, and Cordelia slowed her relentless pace to look down each one, curious about their destinations. She always wanted to go down the road she ought not.

Now Ruby had drawn ahead, keen to reach the town and then get home again, where she would no doubt crawl into a ball and feel sorry for herself. Cordelia wondered whether she should declare that they were to head into Cambridge for a day of shopping.

Now that *would* be unkind.

They began to see more people on the road and in the fields and cottages now, setting up to be about their day of work. There was a gang of navvies up ahead of them, but they turned off along a part-paved toll-road. A farmer in a cart of hay trundled past from behind. Two women and a herd of geese, the birds' feet coated in tar to protect them, stood by the side of the road, talking as the birds milled around, never straying too far, as if held together by an invisible rope strung around them.

Ruby was still a pace ahead of Cordelia now, but she stopped abruptly as a rider on a horse approached them from the town.

"Now there's a pleasing sight," Ruby remarked, and sucked in her belly.

Cordelia clicked her tongue in annoyance but she, too, looked at the dashing figure with appreciation. "Ah," she said. "It is the doctor."

He seemed shabbily dressed, his coat open to show his shirt, and he wore no waistcoat. He was a virile figure, the sort that students would paint in their history paintings at the Academy. He ought to have been wrestling a python not riding a placid chestnut mare.

"Good morning–" Cordelia began but he didn't slow his pace. He half-stood in the stirrups and tipped at his hat, but did not smile nor speak as he trotted briskly past, his eyes already sliding past her to fix upon the horizon beyond. He didn't look at her enough to have recognised her.

"How rude," Ruby said, staring after him, her hands on her hips. "It was as if you were not there."

Cordelia shrugged. "That is most men's reaction to me at my time of life," she said.

"My lady! No, I shall not hear you say that. You have many suitors. You receive so many letters, and callers, too..."

"Only because they believe that I am wealthy. Until that point, of course, I am easily ignored." Although that wasn't exactly true, she had to concede. Her height and her broad shoulders made her stand out even among a group of men. She was noticed ... but rarely considered interesting. Only the temptation of money gave her an attractiveness to a certain type of man. And she had far less than the world liked to suppose.

She wasn't going to brood on it. That solved nothing. Ruby began to say something placatory and untrue, but Cordelia stopped her, saying, "It's perfectly fine, girl. Such invisibility, of a sort, can be a source of amusement." She watched the disappearing figure. "Now, that is interesting. Where do you suppose he is going?"

"To attend a patient," Ruby said. "And that would probably account for his lack of respect to you."

"He was riding with no real haste. He was distracted, not urgent. He has turned left; do you recall that narrow track? I am convinced that it leads nowhere but the river. Did he seem like a fisherman to you?"

"You're right; he seemed like a man preoccupied," Ruby said.

"Indeed. Strange are the ways of men, and country men in particular. Well, let us go on."

The road had no turnpike on this side of town, and they were soon moving along a busier street, where houses crowded together as if there weren't hundreds of acres of open land all about them. In London they were tearing down the worst of the rookeries but here they seemed intent upon all living upon one another's heads.

"You would have no secrets from your neighbours in these parts," Cordelia said to Ruby.

"Indeed not, my lady. But the people here are too poor to have secrets; they barely have bread."

Cordelia looked sideways at the maid, wondering about her background; she had arrived in Cordelia's service with good recommendations but now she was convinced that Ruby's various previous employers had simply been keen to get rid of her. She was about to ask the manner of place Ruby had been born in, and whether she had had much schooling, when screaming and shouting drew her attention to a side street up ahead, on the right.

"Intriguing," Cordelia said and surged towards the noise.

"My lady, no, please. It will be no more than a fight or a drunkard. Come away."

Cordelia strode along, holding her skirts slightly away from her legs with her right hand so that she could walk faster. Her horsehair crin-au-lin was not as large as was currently fashionable – indeed, women's skirts seemed to be expanding by the inch on an hourly basis, if the magazines were to be believed – but if she chanced a run, she feared she would end up in a tangle of fabric. She rounded the corner and found herself at the head of a side street, on her right, that was closed at the end by a high grassy bank and the river, a hundred yards away. Either side of the street were rows of low, mean cottages, joined in a terrace. And partway down, on the left, the rough wooden door of one dwelling stood open, and all the neighbours of the street were standing around, in various states of dress and undress, and from within the house came a long and continual wail.

Cordelia pushed past the stupefied onlookers and reached the door.

CHAPTER TWO

"Send for the constable!" cried a woman who was half as wide as she was tall, with red chapped hands and a face that was mightily familiar with a gin bottle, judging from the veins on her nose and in her pink eyes. "Robert, you must run to the shoe-maker's directly. Run, boy! Get gone." She fetched a solid back-hander across the head of a ragged-haired boy who ducked under it with a practised movement. He launched himself out of the dark cottage room, barging past Cordelia with his sharp elbows akimbo.

Cordelia stepped fully into the square room, holding her breath, and looked around. It was not her usual haunt and she was curious. Even when she'd made visits to the poor around her own estate, she had stayed away from the meanest of hovels. She had been taught to try to distinguish between the deserving poor, and the rest; it had something to do with how often a wife cleaned the doorstep, apparently.

This doorstep was grubby.

But everyone else was gawping, so why not me, she decided when she entered. It was an unremarkable and bare place; the windows were very small, and unlike the step they were polished clean, but the light was filtered through yellowing curtains which were pulled across the rippled glass and it cast a dank atmosphere on the few pieces of solid dark furniture. There were three empty chairs by the fire, though they did not match and one had a missing arm. Along one wall, an open fire with the semblance of a range stood cold and unlit. *There was no way of baking there*, she thought as she looked, but a cauldron hung on a hook and a toasting-fork was propped by the wood basket. *And no coal.* But no doubt the occupant got by well enough.

Narrow stairs led up from the left, and on the back wall there was a door that led out into another room.

And there was the figure of a man, a solid and fleshy sort, lying on the floor with his legs and arms at angles that spoke of ominous deeds. Yet it was not he that was attracting the greatest attention. There was a woman sitting on the fourth wooden chair in the centre of the room, and her sounds varied from wild screaming until they peaked at a high keening before fading to low sobbing for a few seconds, then returning once more to its unholy crescendo. The woman who had ordered the boy out of the cottage was now by her side, one chapped hand firmly on the seated woman's shoulder, holding her down on the chair. The woman might have been wailing in fear, or simply in frustration at being held down.

"Mrs Hurrell, calm yourself and we shall presently have the answer." The speaker didn't have an ounce of sympathy in her rough voice. "Robert will be along with the constable as soon as he may."

"But call for the doctor!" the seated woman cried. She had tears running down her face but she was frowning too; there was anger there, and confusion, as much as fear. "What use is the constable? Thomas needs attention; let me go to him. You cannot let him lie there."

"I'm afraid there is nothing a doctor might do for him now, Mrs Hurrell. No, you stay sitting."

Mrs Hurrell, the crying woman, had been trying to stand but the other woman's hand upon her shoulder was clearly heavy and firm. Mrs Hurrell subsided back into the chair and glared around.

There were a half dozen other people crowded into the cottage, and though a few slid curious sideways glances at Cordelia in her fine dark gown, most were transfixed by the spectacle in front of them. All had seen gentry in their time, usually at a distance, and everyone had encountered injury and death, but not all had seen a scene with drama like this, and it was currently the greater attraction.

"My lady!" Ruby pushed through from behind and came to Cordelia's side, gasping as she saw the prone figure. "Oh my … is that blood? He looks … Oh, look at his head! No!"

Cordelia peered and leaned forward as her eyes adjusted to the gloom. The young man lay on his back, his arms up as if he had fallen with his hands in the air. His head was wrenched most awkwardly to one side, and a spreading dark stain issued from the back of his matted head. His eyes were open, and unblinking.

"Oh…" Ruby moaned. She half-turned but there were more people pressing in from outside, and seeing she was trapped, instead she panicked and bolted for the one clear exit that she could see, the door at the back of the room.

"I must have water…"

Cordelia didn't think she'd find a pump out at the back but she let the maid go. She was more concerned with the apparent lack of direction being shown by any of the crowd of neighbours.

"Why did you send for a shoemaker as well as the constable?" she demanded in the most authoritative voice she could; an easy task, of course, and one she had been bred to.

The woman with the red, chapped hands - a laundress, Cordelia decided - blinked in surprise but answered automatically, as she too had been bred to do. "The shoemaker *is* the constable," she said. "It is George Bell in these parts. He undertakes the office on a part-time basis."

"Have you no county police force?"

The woman looked a little blank. "We're not like fancy towns," she said. "Not here. It's not compulsory, is it?" She started to look around at the others, hoping for help.

Cordelia was not going to let things slide. "Well, whatever it is that you have here, a constable is a start but more is needed to be done. The doctor does need to be called."

"But he's dead," the laundress said, setting off a fresh wail of anguish and anger from the seated Mrs Hurrell. "Our doctor is good, I'm sure, but of no use to this one now. He does not re-animate dead flesh!"

"Yes, I can see that, but there are procedures," Cordelia said. She turned around and there was no need for her to push through the onlookers; the crowd seemed to part as she made her way towards the door. She poked her head out and beckoned a likely-looking boy of around twelve. "You. Do you know the doctor? Doctor Arnall?"

"Yes, madam."

"Do you want to earn a penny?"

"Yes, please, madam." His eyes shone.

"You must fetch him directly. This is a matter of life and death. Well, death, at any rate."

The young lad set off but as he got to the top of the street, he turned to the right to head into town, and Cordelia let loose a bellow that threatened to burst her corset: "Wait, boy!"

He stopped, as did every other person on the street and a passing cart too.

"I have seen him this morning, going the other way,"

she shouted, pointing frantically to the left.

"His house lies this way," the boy called back.

"He is not at his house, then," she shouted. "Go the other way, and turn left again, to the river." After a moment of indecision, the boy turned about and set off in the other direction.

Sighing, Cordelia re-entered the cottage. It seemed as if no one had moved, and now a curious silence had descended, provoked by her alarming and unladylike hollering. Everyone stared but as soon as she met their eyes, they dropped their gazes. No one knew who she was but her status was apparent, and it paralysed them with indecision.

"I have sent for the doctor," she said, rather superfluously. Everyone in town was probably aware of her summons. "Things have to be done, you know. There are declarations to be made, paperwork to be signed, that sort of thing. Who is this man, anyway?"

Feet shuffled and eyes were lowered even further. All she could see was a sea of hair and bald spots. Hats were clutched in front of bodies like shields. Eventually the laundress spoke up. "That there unfortunate is Thomas

Bains. He was a lodger here. He had the back room."

"I see. And is he prone to fights, perhaps? Was there an altercation here?"

Mrs Hurrell started up again, blurting out the words in a staccato burst of phlegm and tears. "This is my house. My house. He was my lodger. Just my lodger. I came home and he was like that, he was. You ain't no call to make me sit here like this." She struggled against the laundress's hand.

"Came home?" Cordelia said. "You were abroad early. Industrious woman…" *Or she had been out all night, perhaps.*

A man found his voice. "You see! It is a likely tale, is it not! She has no cause to be out from this house. She killed him more like, and now is pretending that she happened upon his body. Look at her!"

"No, no! Why should I kill him?" Mrs Hurrell's eyes were narrowed now.

"Why should you not?" the man spat back. "I can think of a hundred reasons you would kill him, and one hundred and one is simply for spite. A woman of your past, eh? London ways, that's what it is! We all know of your *London ways*. Anyways, 'tis common knowledge that a lad like that had it coming."

"Don't you speak ill of the dead!" a woman called from behind, interrupting Cordelia's query as to what sort of lad a "lad like that" was, and what "London ways" might be. She had no chance to repeat the question as the people in the room stepped aside to let a new man enter.

"I have been sent for," said the grey-haired man, looking around with wide pale eyes. "But the boy made no sense. Mrs Hurrell – Oh!" He stepped back. He was wearing a plain working man's garb of sober brown trousers and a shirt and beige waistcoat, but he must have only just risen, as he still carried his coat upon his arm as if he had left the house in a hurry and dressed upon the journey. She wondered if this was the shoemaker-constable, and judged from the callouses and marks on his hands that he probably was. His waistcoat showed a sharp, deep crease all around his waist where she imagined an apron was habitually tied. He had a nose that looked like it had been pinched with pliers and then drawn out longer.

"Oh!" he repeated again, and looked around with desperation in his eyes. "That is Thomas. What has happened?"

"Surely you are the one to discover that," the laundress

said, a sneer hiding in her voice. "Here is Mrs Hurrell, who claims to have found the body yet she was not raising the alarm until I came in to see her and found her lying by the door, crying and going on, most unseemly like."

"Oh!" said the shoemaker-constable again. "Oh." Cordelia was beginning to doubt the man's wits. *Was the office of constable passed around between village simpletons?*

Cordelia took charge. She couldn't bear not to. She was mistress at home, after all. So she would be mistress here. "I have sent for the doctor," she informed the gibbering shoemaker-constable.

The man glanced at the prone figure, blanched and looked away, licking his lips. "But I fear it might be too late…" he whispered.

Cordelia sighed. "I also believe you now need to inform the coroner," she said. "As is the standard practice in all cases of unexplained death."

"Do I? Is it?"

"Yes, you do. Listen, man. I might not be a constable … or, indeed, a shoemaker … but I read a great deal of novels of the more lurid type, and I know the procedure. You must send word to the coroner and probably the sheriff or whoever it is that keeps order in this county."

"We share a sheriff with Huntingdonshire," the man said, as if that were a reason to not call upon him.

"Then go and persuade Huntingdonshire to relinquish him for a while," she snapped back. "Now clear this room, keep Mrs Hurrell here seated, and will someone find a sheet to afford the dead man a little dignity?"

She clapped her hands, and the townsfolk responded.

Chapter Three

By the time the doctor arrived, someone had fetched a rough blanket to drape over the dead man, but Cordelia stepped in to prevent anyone from moving him. The red-faced laundress shot her an openly venomous look when Cordelia ordered her to leave the young man's limbs as they were, but she did not argue back. A stiff and curious silence fell upon the assembled crowd within the cottage as the shoemaker-constable went outside to dither and panic and organise messengers. She followed, to linger by the door and listen to proceedings.

She was pleased to hear him following her suggestions on who needed to be sent for. She overheard someone say, "That doctor will be out in a field somewhere, his head in the soil and his bottom in the air! I seen him last week, you know. Like dancing, but not natural."

"Callis-fennis," someone else said. "All that stretching his bits with no coat on. For shame."

There was a ripple of laughter, hastily suppressed when the constable said, "Show some respect! A man lies dead within." Silence fell outside, matching the expectant quiet inside the cottage.

Cordelia was loath to leave the scene. She knew her presence was having a repressive effect on the gawpers, and in that sense she was probably doing some good. She felt, very keenly, that no one ought to be meddling with things until persons of a more knowledgeable sort arrived. She had heard of deaths in London and other places where enterprising souls had sold tickets for people to view the body. She was determined that it should not happen here.

She had tried to make polite conversation while they waited, but no one had much to say beyond "I don't know, madam" and "Well, he was a young man, so…" and then they would peter out, as if their half-sentence conveyed everything that needed to be said.

She heard the doctor arrive by the flurry of voices and the sound of a horse's hooves stirring up small stones outside. She could not resist smiling and adopting an air of casual insouciance in reply to his somewhat startled greeting as he dipped inside the cottage and saw her.

"Lady Cornbrook! Good morning. I had not expected to see you here."

"Of course," she said, her enigmatic non-answer being her slight revenge at his lack of courtesy when they had met on the road not half an hour before. He hadn't been home to dress more decently, she noted. His usually bouncy, wavy hair hung in lank locks from below his top hat, almost as if it were wet or soaked with sweat. He swung the hat from his head as he remembered his courtesies.

She nodded, and waved her hand towards the body. "I had them leave him exactly as he fell."

"Indeed. Well, er, thank you for that," he said, and paused for a moment. He clutched at his black shoulder bag, and looked around the room, blinking as his eyes adjusted. "Might we have more light in here? Anyone?"

The doctor went forward to the body and knelt down, setting his hat at some distance away so the blood would not encroach on it. The laundress crossed to the windows and pulled aside the yellowing curtains, and someone else lit a lamp which smoked and smelled. Now that the doctor was about his business, people began to crowd in from outside to watch him work. Cordelia looked for the shoemaker-constable but he was standing behind a knot of men, wringing his hands.

"The doctor needs light!" Cordelia announced. "And air! *Constable*, might you urge these people outside?"

The crowds reluctantly left, more under her direction than that of the constable until only five persons and the dead man remained. The constable stood by the door, trying to look anywhere but at the floor where the doctor was examining the corpse closely.

Mrs Hurrell was still seated, and the laundress had, in an unexpected move of pity, brought her a cup of hot tea. Mrs Hurrell had it clamped in her shaking hands, barely seeming able to take a sip.

Cordelia, unlike the constable, could not tear her eyes from the doctor's task. She had been staying at Hugo Hawke's country estate for only a few days, but she had already met the doctor at a dinner that Hugo had held to announce her arrival; he had been seated some distance from her, and appeared not to talk with any great animation to the others around him. She had heard he was married, but on that evening he had arrived unaccompanied. Beardless and in his thirties, with a smooth face and curling dark hair, he was a good looking man but she had yet to see him smile. It didn't matter. She wanted to like him because he seemed the opposite in his manner and deportment to her late husband.

He knelt with his back to her, now, and had put his jacket to one side. His shirt was damp, clinging to his lean body in a way that suggested very great exertion, as if he had sweated from every pore. That, or he had been caught in a downpour. She realised that she was staring at the outline of his torso with more attention than was seemly, and tore her gaze away, meeting instead the worried eyes of the constable by the door.

"Ought you not come forward and learn about the manner of his death?" Cordelia said. Trying to be kind, she took a step towards the body, to encourage him. "You will find clues as to the perpetrator. It is not so very alarming a sight; come. You will have seen such things before."

The constable made a strangled noise but he approached, warily. He glanced at the body, at the sticky blood that reflected the weak light of the lamp that had been placed on the floor, and at the doctor whose hands were probing into the back of the skull. The doctor pulled aside a hairy flap of skin, exposing some white bone, and the constable whimpered. He swallowed noisily and she could see that he was no longer focusing. He tipped his head back and stared fixedly at the wall.

Cordelia saw the young man on the floor as a person, but she found she was able to put it to one side as she peered down. She had had a rigorous upbringing which included a great deal of household management skills. Her parents had acknowledged that she was not a great beauty, and had often reminded her that a successful marriage was going to rely on her talents rather than her looks. If she could not assess a well-hung deer or prepare a chicken, then she was likely to be fleeced by her staff. They never intended that she ever *cook* in her own kitchen - no, a gently-bred Englishwoman was supposed to leave such things to the strange Continentals - but she had to know what occurred there.

Although, in defiance of convention, Cordelia had taken a more practical role in many instances. For many months, the kitchen in her marital home had been a place of refuge that the finer rooms had not offered.

So, looking at the sorry mess, she tuned out the emotion attached to the scene and saw, instead, the mere flesh and bone from which the spirit had fled. "See, there," she said to the unwilling constable. "He has taken a blow to the left side of his face. I would imagine that it sent him flying backwards. He would have hit his head on the corner of that sideboard. Doctor, what say you? Is the wound on the back of his skull as if he had struck the angle of the wood?"

"It is," the doctor acknowledged without looking up from his work. He turned the corpse's head from one side to the other, so that they could better see the reddened mark on the left cheek.

"A left-handed blow," Cordelia said again, and could not prevent herself looking at Mrs Hurrell as she brought her tea to her lips. The woman's right hand was shaking and the tea was as much on her skirts as in the cup.

Then she looked back at the doctor, who was making a note in a small book, and he stopped suddenly and turned to glance over his shoulder at her. He put his pen down and turned back to the corpse.

He was left-handed.

Cordelia shook her head, mostly in reproach to herself. *No, come now*, she thought. *I saw him riding away. He has been sweating – or washing himself. He seems an uncommon sort. Oh, that would be rather too neat, would it not?*

CHAPTER FOUR

The constable was not faring well. She could hear his laboured breathing and when she turned, she saw that he was sheened with sweat and pointing his prominent nose determinedly into the corner of the room as if he might see a confession written upon the peeling wallpaper.

Divining that he needed direction, she stepped back and he followed, automatically. She said, "I am always fascinated by crime and criminals. Why, I take all the London papers so that I might follow the famous trials. I imagine that next, you will be talking to all people present while things are fresh in their minds. Am I right?"

She hoped that she presented herself as a mere dilettante, wanting to learn from a real policeman, but the constable's face didn't exactly glow with pride. Mind you, she had to concede that she had been an unsuccessful coquette even when in the blooming rosiness of youth. Where the other girls at her finishing school could persuade any gentleman to do almost anything, she had mostly relied upon challenging them to arm-wrestling matches and poker games. She excelled at both. Neither seemed like a good option at this moment. The constable licked his lips nervously and tipped his head to her in awkward respect.

"I believe that I will, I mean, I should, I shall," he stammered. "I, my paper, my books, I mean..." He spread his hands wide. "In my haste, I..."

Goodness, but the man was worse than useless. She kept her face politely impassive and screamed internally, a skill that she imagined was learned by all women of all classes. She went towards the sideboard that ranged along one wall, skirting around the prone figure. The shelves of the upper portion held a mismatched array of crockery and pans, but there were drawers above the lower cupboards. She glanced towards Mrs Hurrell.

"Madam, might you have any paper upon which the constable could write?" she asked hopefully. "An envelope or some brown parcel paper should do."

Mrs Hurrell's blurry face was crumpled and she hung

her head, shaking it dolefully from side to side. "No, ma'am, I fear not." She rolled her eyes heavenwards. "Why must this have all happened to me?"

It has actually happened to the young man, Cordelia thought. She let her hand stray towards the nearest drawer, which was partly open. "But I see here, within–"

"No! You must not touch that!" Mrs Hurrell cried out, rising to her feet. The china cup tumbled from her hand and smashed on the floor, and immediately the laundress was by Mrs Hurrell's side, and pressing her back to her chair once more. Mrs Hurrell flung up her hands in protest but she submitted. Her face was thunderous and her eyes wide.

Cordelia withdrew her hand and gave the constable a hard stare, trying to convey to him the importance of Mrs Hurrell's fiery reaction. The constable was slack-jawed and confused, but he showed a spark of promise by suddenly declaring that he would go out to send a boy to his house to collect his official notebook. In truth he probably wanted to be out of the cottage, and he left before anyone could protest.

Cordelia rocked on her heels and looked towards the drawer once more, trying to peep at the cream papers within. There was a folded newspaper, its tiny print crammed onto the large sheets in long columns, but she could not determine the name.

Mrs Hurrell was still in the throes of hysterics where anger and fear warred, and she was jabbering, "I swear, I do swear, before God and all the angels, I had nothing to do with this! I was sent a note and I went out and when I came back, there he was! Dead! And I felt a great heaviness wash over me and I fell, I did, I swear, and all was black and I was crying until Mrs Kale found me."

The laundress, now identified as Mrs Kale, tutted. "And why did you not call for help?"

"Mrs Kale, you know me, you have known me these past eight years that I have lived here! I was quite overcome with the shock. The blood. His arms. His arms, oh, did you not see how he lay? I am not a delicate woman, as you know, but it was too much."

Mrs Hurrell was sitting once more in her chair, and bending forward, her back quite straight by virtue of her solid and decent undergarments but her shoulders were sagging and her neck arched over so that her head was clasped in her veined and wrinkled hands. *There was still a great strength in her,* Cordelia thought as she looked at the women. *Not a delicate woman, no.* Her neck had the ropes of muscle that belonged to a strong working woman. Her feet were planted squarely apart, and her figure was substantial without being indolent.

She was, Cordelia thought, *as capable as anyone else of landing a blow upon a man's face, her current aspect of despair notwithstanding. And that despair was shaded with other emotions.*

"How old was Thomas Bains?" Cordelia asked.

The doctor was engrossed in his work and did not reply. Mrs Hurrell stifled a sob or a groan at the mention of the deceased's name, and Mrs Kale folded her arms and sniffed. No one seemed willing to speak. Cordelia was aware that her presence was deeply unwelcome but no one had the spirit to tell her to leave.

"He looks as if he is in his early twenties," Cordelia prompted.

"Around that," Mrs Kale muttered at last.

"And he lived here with Mrs Hurrell?"

That insinuation was enough to prompt a sudden flux of information from the curious woman on the seat. "He was my lodger. He took the back room, with his father,

43

God rest his soul. Near on six years they have been there. They *had* been there."

"His late father?"

"Yes, old Maurice. The pair of them lived there. Till his father's death, just last year."

"And did Thomas work? Had he a trade?" Cordelia insisted.

Mrs Hurrell dried up. She kept her face hidden. Finally Mrs Kale stepped in. "He was employed from time to time, up at the big house for Mr Hawke, but only in the gardens, on account of…"

"…on account of…?"

"Well, he were a nice enough lad and I cannot speak ill of the dead, you know. He did try. But he was the clumsiest man you ever did meet, and his mouth clumsier than his body, if you see what I mean."

Cordelia wasn't sure she did see. "Do you mean to say that he was rude? Tactless, perhaps?"

"Ahh, he was a loud and boastful sort. The thing is, though, I don't believe he meant anything by it. He just could not be silent when he did ought to be silent, that was all. If you said to him, sit, he would want to know why."

"I see." Cordelia studied the body where it lay. *Clumsy? Had he simply fallen?* The reddened mark on his cheek could have been obtained earlier - the previous night, perhaps, in a brawl outside a beerhouse.

"Doctor," she said. "Can you tell how old the bruise upon his cheek is?"

"Not with any great accuracy," he admitted. "The coroner is expert in these matters. Indeed, I am done here. My skill does not extend to this sort of case." He began to pack away his things. "I have made notes as to the exact marks upon the body. In the event that the coroner is delayed, he will be able to refer to my notes. But as to any kind of diagnosis, that is not for me to say." He got to his feet, pulled on his coat, and picked up his leather bag and hat. He turned to her and spoke as if to an equal, as if he addressed a man. "However, I would suggest that the bruise does not look like an old one."

"Might it have been inflicted last night?" Cordelia pressed.

"I would not say so. It has not yet darkened. As time passes, the blood will pool and congeal."

"I see," she said, fascinated. She wanted to ask if that

45

was the same process in a dead body as a live one, but stopped herself. The doctor was making a move to leave, and he paused by the door to look back at her.

He flipped back to standard social propriety. "Lady Cornbrook, might I escort you to a place more becoming to your station? I would be delighted to take you back to Wallerton Manor. The events of this morning must have been rather traumatic for you."

Dashed exciting more like, she thought, *and more interesting than needlework*, but she didn't want to scandalise the man. With a polite smile she shook her head. "Have no care for me, doctor," she said. "But I thank you for your kindness. My maid is somewhere at the back of this house and she will see me to safety, I have no doubt. You have work to do and I would not delay you."

She expected a protest and a few minutes of tedious to-and-fro, as society usually demanded, but he nodded and simply left, calling for the constable to return to his post within the cottage as he did so.

Cordelia was still reluctant to leave. This was the most interesting thing to have happened for many years. She wondered if she could lurk in the shadows even as the coroner and perhaps the sheriff went about their business. Though if they were coming from any great distance, it would be some time before they arrived.

The constable coughed.

She ignored him, and went through the door at the back of the room, saying to no one in particular, "I shall go and find my maid."

CHAPTER FIVE

"Well, Ruby, I think little of the police authorities in this area," Cordelia declared.

Ruby's shoulders jerked in surprise and she looked up. She was sitting on a wooden box, her back against the rear wall of the small enclosed yard. She was about to get to her feet, but Cordelia waved her down again.

The back room that she had passed through – the apparent residence of Thomas Bains – had been a dark and cold abode. It made the front room of the cottage look palatial. There was a long, low bed under the window, covered in a mess of crumpled grey blankets that had hairy, unbound edges and greasy stains. By another wall stood a table and one wooden ladder-back chair with broken rungs. On the table was a lamp and an empty bottle, and on a shelf there ranged a collection of tins and pots; hair cream, a rolled-up pair of braces, and some mustard powder in a yellow packet. The air smelled of turpentine and staleness. She did not linger in the small room, but instead passed through quickly in search of her unwell maid.

Ruby was looking a little better, and there was colour now in her pale cheeks. "What is going on in there, my lady?" she asked.

"Foul play, for certain," Cordelia said, "and regrettably I have little confidence that the man in there, the constable, has any clue what to do about it."

"Foul play? Do you mean to say, murder?"

"That is exactly what I mean," Cordelia said, a thrill running through her. "But they say they have no county police force here, and instead cling to the old ways, with part time parish constables and watch committees, I suppose, and the like. The man in charge of bringing criminals to justice is nothing but a grey little shoemaker, and even the doctor, good man that I am sure he is, could not speak with certainty about the death."

"It will just have been a fight," Ruby said, shaking her head. "He is a young man. It is a common enough thing, and likely the constable and the doctor have seen it before."

"The constable must be new, or have no stomach for it, or something," Cordelia said. "Or maybe nothing ever happens here. He has not seen the marks of violence like that before, poor man."

"Nor have I," Ruby pointed out. "Nothing quite so ... bloody, at any rate."

Cordelia felt a sudden pang of responsibility. Still, no one could get through life without seeing a goodly share of death, and she didn't suppose that it was the first corpse the young woman had seen. The only difference was that this one was not nicely presented in a casket, and had rather a deal more blood scattered about. "The fight was recent," she said, pensively. "This was no late-night beerhouse brawl. It happened early this morning."

Ruby was unimpressed by the deductions of her mistress. "Last night's arguments can become this morning's revenge," she said. "Who was the woman who was crying and shouting? His mother?"

"No; his landlady. He rents this back room from her. There is suspicion upon her, too, as she was found in the room, lying against the wall rather than seeking help. She is in a strange state, halfway between fear and anger."

"That sounds more like self-defence than murder, then," Ruby said. "We women know that state very well."

Cordelia realised what the young woman was suggesting. "Oh. No, I cannot countenance that. He is young, and she is old, after all."

Ruby raised one delicate eyebrow. "Now, my lady, if I were to suggest that an older woman could not be attractive to a younger man…"

Cordelia was surprised at the maid offering such an unsought opinion. It wouldn't do. But she answered, anyway. "Yes, yes, quite. However, in this case, I feel it is unlikely."

"In life, many things are," Ruby said, pushing her luck. "People do find themselves attracted to the strangest things. In Covent Garden once, I met a man who said that his master liked his mistress to dress as a … ah. Forgive me." She stuttered and looked down.

"Oh, discretion be damned," Cordelia said, her smile wide and unladylike, delighted and scandalised in equal measure. "Tell me. What did this master do?"

But Ruby had flamed red with embarrassment at having been caught speaking with her mistress almost as a confidante. She shook her head, mutely.

Cordelia sighed. She had a good imagination. "Without a dynamic constable, this murder will go unpunished," she said. "I ought to take charge."

Ruby stifled a snort of surprise. "My lady, please. You have no experience or qualifications in such matters."

"Nor does the shoemaker."

"He does," Ruby said. "For he is a man."

That was a truth so obvious it didn't warrant a reply. Instead, Cordelia paced the few square yards of the walled enclosure. "Oh, Ruby, you are new to my service. But you must understand this about me. I need something to occupy my mind. I read books about this sort of crime, and I know I can discover the truth. I long for a challenge, a new direction, a release. Do you not see? Even if I were to follow the case from the side, as it were, in parallel with the official investigation, that would be something." Even as she spoke, she felt unladylike enthusiasm rise up and make her skin tingle. "I simply want to know the outcome."

"My lady, with respect, I understand that you have had many such projects." Ruby spoke with a hint of exasperation in her voice. Cordelia added "cheek and back-chat" to her mental list of her maid's probable deficiencies, though she wasn't as offended by them as she thought she probably ought to be.

Ruby was continuing. "I had heard that you tried your hand at writing romances, did you not? And articles for the press, under other names, of course. And then there was local history, and botany, and was there not also a book of manners—"

"Enough!" Cordelia was shocked that Ruby knew so much of her sad, and failed, activities. But of course, Ruby would have discovered the rooms in the house where the copies of her books were stacked up, printed and bound at her own expense, and where they were now languishing in dusty piles.

Each one was a symbol of a past enthusiasm that came to nothing as she tried to fill her life with something more meaningful than deciding on dinner choices in a vast and empty house; her home, that would soon not even be her home any longer.

Ruby cowered back and Cordelia remembered that for all her outspokenness, she was as yet unused to Cordelia's ways and could not be sure that Cordelia would not take a rod to her, as was her right as Mistress. Cordelia spread her open hands wide and smiled. "Come now, Ruby. I speak harshly; I apologise. Yes, I have dabbled but this is something far more exciting than my poor treatises on the flowering plants of southern England. This is for *justice*."

At least that book about flowers had been ignored, she thought. Her book of manners had been seized upon by the press in a dry season devoid of real news, and for a painful few weeks she had been reviewed, pilloried and generally humiliated for her attempts to draw up a new code of conduct for men and women.

Enough, she told herself, as she had told Ruby. A widowed woman might be allowed her idiosyncrasies, and all manner of deviations could be expressed in the aftermath of tragedy and grief. Others sought it in gin or opiates or affairs. There was no harm in this.

Even if, as in her case, her particular past tragedy had had two results and one was that of release.

"Maybe you are right," Cordelia said at last. It was nothing to do with her. "It will have been nothing more than a fight, and a sad end to it. Poor man. We should get back. They will have missed us at breakfast, by now."

Ruby accepted Cordelia's outstretched hand and rose to her feet, taking a moment to smooth down her skirts and arrange her bonnet. As she moved away from the wooden box that had served as her seat, something caught Cordelia's eye.

"Did you move the box, girl?" she asked.

Ruby turned to look. "No, it was placed just there when I came out."

"Indeed." Cordelia pointed to the floor of the yard. It was made of bricks, laid in a haphazard manner, many of them cracked and broken by frost and ill-use. Packed down hard on top was dust and dirt, and she imagined that in wet weather, the yard was an unpleasant morass. "Look. The box had originally stood by the back door, where you can see the deep ruts at the corners. But it has been dragged across to the wall." She pointed to the fresh grooves in the dust.

"Well, not by me," Ruby said disdainfully. She wouldn't move herself if she didn't have to; dragging a box was well out of her range.

Cordelia eyed the wall. It was nearly six feet high, she judged. Would a fit man be able to climb such a wall? It was a rough wall of stones and rocks, unplastered, with crannies for potential footholds. She gathered up her skirts and jumped onto the box so that she could peer over the top of the wall. Her petticoats were pushed flat against her thighs and billowed out stiffly behind.

"I would lay a wager that whoever did the evil deed in there, that they made their escape this way and scaled the wall, using the box to help themselves climb. Perhaps they were short. Perhaps they were simply unused to such exercise. Or hampered in some way. What do you think? Could you climb this wall, Ruby?"

"Certainly not!"

"Well, I think that I might," Cordelia said. She raised her arms, and her tight bodice pinched and pulled. But she took a deep breath, found a hand-hold, and hauled hard as she could with her arms.

CHAPTER SIX

Cordelia's upper body strength had not diminished since the active days of her girlhood. She had retained a keen interest in tending to her gardens, and enjoyed outdoor pursuits such as riding and carriage-driving. She did not tend towards the growing new fashion to lace one's corset tighter and tighter; all the best doctors were warning against the practise, and she was inclined to agree. So she retained a degree of movement that meant she could continue being scandalously mobile.

After her marriage, she had plunged into an active role in managing the gardens and estates around her new home. To the constant consternation of her cook, Mrs Unsworth, she also gravitated to the kitchens where, against all convention, she would embark on unbecoming physical tasks such as kneading great loaves of bread or stripping down carcasses for the lard that nestled in white layers below the skin of animals. There was some strange release to be found in the activity of the body, Cordelia found. After the – *unfortunate* – death of her husband, when the world seemed to crowd in around her and press down upon her throat and mouth in layers of suffocating black crape, she had rebelled and sought solace in the pure act of simply *moving*. It reminded her that she was alive.

More alive than before.

She pushed the maudlin thoughts aside and concentrated on her task.

And the muscles gained through such misadventures served her well now. She hauled hard with her arms, ignoring the tearing of her bodice stitching, and swung her legs up to one side, caring not that her petticoats were now displayed. She had taken to wearing the new bloomers, for warmth, and it had become a habit even in summer. Now she was glad of it. With an effort, and an indelicate grunt, she hooked her right ankle on the top of the wall. Her left foot found purchase in a deep crevasse and she was able, then, to lever herself up. She had no time to gather her thoughts; with a cry she could not suppress, she found herself on a trajectory that sent her over the wall and tumbling down the other side, to land in a spiky mess of dry weeds, wilting grass and a few unwelcome nettles.

"Mistress! My lady! Lady Cornbrook!" Ruby screamed in panic.

Cordelia sat up and was, for once, grateful for the layers of clothing that was a woman's lot in life to haul around. They had protected her from the worst ravages of the stone wall and the scrub in which she now sat. "Ruby, I am unharmed," she called. She got to her feet and saw Ruby's bonnet poking above the wall, her white-gloved hands scrabbling along the top edge.

To Cordelia's delight and surprise, Ruby managed to scale the wall, her once-pale face now red and blotchy with effort. She got herself atop it, and sat, looking down. "Oh. Now I am stuck."

"Jump," Cordelia said, extending her hands.

Ruby closed her eyes and let herself fall forwards, landing in the flattened patch of nettles that Cordelia had just vacated. She shrieked and looked up. "I thought you were to catch me!"

"I did not say so, girl," Cordelia replied with a shrug.

"One ought not make assumptions. A lesson learned. Are you hurt?"

"No, my lady."

"Good. Well, then. On your feet, girl."

Ruby snatched up her bonnet and scowled crossly, another note to be added to Cordelia's mental list of the maid's less desirable qualities, diverting though they sometimes were. Cordelia studied the place they now found themselves in. Due to the slope of the land, it would be almost impossible to return to the yard the way they had come; they were lower this side than the level of the yard on the other side of the wall. They were on the bank of the river, a grassy patch about eight feet wide that faded from earth to reeds and then to water by unremarkable degrees.

She looked up and down but there was trampled vegetation in both directions; no doubt it was a cut-through from place to place that avoided the turnpikes, or perhaps fishermen came this way. At any rate, she could not tell which way the murderer might have escaped. Left and right looked the same. She had hoped clues would leap out at her. Nothing did.

"Come, Ruby, let us find our way back to the cottage."

"Are we not going back to the manor? Breakfast, my lady…"

Well, at least the girl's hangover had cleared. "In good time."

* * *

They tramped through the grass and weeds, Cordelia occasionally stopping to point out a particularly interesting plant or flower to Ruby, who muttered under her breath and was no longer even pretending to be polite. In light of the unusual circumstances, Cordelia decided not to reprimand the girl. Ruby was a town-dweller, Cordelia understood, and from her stream of half-heard invectives, not used to the countryside and its smells, creatures, crawling things and stinging plants.

They came at last to a gap in the wall and followed the narrow passageway to a back street of the town. From there they could hear the sounds of carts and business, and soon they were on the same road by which they had approached earlier. Cordelia led the way, retracing her steps to the row of cottages. The crowd outside had diminished now, with most decent people having jobs to attend to. There were a handful of boys, daring one another to peep in through the window or open the door, but periodically the constable would poke his head out and roar at them to be gone.

When he saw Cordelia and Ruby approaching once more, his face fell and his tone quietened. He came out of the house fully, and pulled the door closed behind him. "Madam," he said stiffly. "We await the coroner, as you yourself directed, and no one is to disturb the scene."

"I left something within," Cordelia lied quickly, smiling sweetly.

"Tell me what it is, and I shall fetch it for you. We hold the suspected murderer here, you see, and cannot be..."

"I think you do not," Cordelia said. "If you mean Mrs Hurrell, I suggest that you are mistaken."

There were the sounds of altercation from inside the cottage. Cordelia could hear Mrs Hurrell begin to shout, "Is that the authorities? Tell them I am innocent and I am being held against my will! Mrs Kale, I shall–"

Then there was the sound of Mrs Kale, gruffly answering with a foul word and an instruction to sit down. The constable spun around and opened the door, shouting for them both to return to their places. Cordelia took her chance and pushed in alongside the constable, who was so afraid of being seen to harm a woman of some status that he shrank away from her rather than push her back into the street.

"It is not the authorities, not I," Cordelia said. "But I do believe that the murderer escaped out of the back of the cottage."

"I have looked," the constable said, his body deferent but his voice betraying his annoyance. "There is nothing but a yard out there, and no means of exit."

"But as you can see," Cordelia said, "both my maid and I *did* escape that way, and so did the murderer. If we can do it, so might anyone. There is a wooden box which has been dragged from its usual position, and used as a step to facilitate his flight over the wall. He had fled by the banks of the river. Have you more men at your disposal? I would suggest a search in both directions."

"I have no men," the constable said, "and no authority to call any, myself. And it is likely that any search would be too late now. In any case, we have the perpetrator here before us. It is as plain as day. Her reactions switch from hysteria to panic to a strange calm from moment to moment. And then she calls up dire threats of violence such as a woman ought not to utter. She is not of a sound mind."

"Good heavens, man. Upon discovering the body of your dead lodger, do you not think your own reactions would be deranged? In my experience–" She stopped herself abruptly. This was not the time to talk of her own experiences. They were not pleasant.

The constable paid no heed, though she knew Ruby would have filed the slip of phrase away.

In the short silence that followed, Mrs Hurrell said loudly, "All murderers must have a motive, do they not? So, then, why would I kill him? What would be my motive? My own lodger, who paid me rent? I would not kill him. He is of far more use to me alive than dead."

Mrs Kale was still standing by, looking like a person employed to keep the peace at a public rally. She put her hands on her hips and tutted. "Oh, do not seek to pull the wool over the eyes of these good people, you old trout," she said, with venom. "These walls are not so thick as you might suppose. I know that he did not pay you as much rent as you thought you could obtain by letting the room out to others. You wanted rid of him, so that you could have three or four railwaymen sleeping there, and charge each one what you got from Thomas alone."

"That is a lie," Mrs Hurrell said, and Cordelia saw a flash of anger in her red-rimmed eyes. Yes, the woman had a strength in her, though from what past Cordelia could not guess.

"There is much about you that is not the truth," Mrs Kale hissed.

Mrs Hurrell opened and closed her mouth, stared around the room in a sudden frenzy, and then burst into a fresh fit of angry tears. Mrs Kale made no move to comfort her. Cordelia wanted to go to her, lay a hand on her shoulder, and assure her that everything would work out and justice would inevitably prevail.

Then Mrs Hurrell plunged a hand into the folded, greasy depths of her gown, and withdrew a yellowed handkerchief. She blew her nose, noisily, and with a start Cordelia realised that she was using her left hand this time, not the right hand that she had drunk her tea with.

Was she truly the innocent party, and sunken deep in distraught shock, or was she indeed a clever woman simply playing a part, and – in fact – the cause of all the current dismay?

CHAPTER SEVEN

Ewatt Carter-Hall was a loud, middle-aged man of means, with a laugh so rich that it couldn't help but force a smile onto the face of anyone who heard it. He called at Wallerton Manor around mid-afternoon, and discovered Cordelia sitting quietly under a parasol on a terrace overlooking the lawns. He was pursued by an aging butler who had three brown teeth in his unsmiling head. The skeletal butler was protesting with restrained outrage that the master of the house, Hugo Hawke, was called away on business for a few hours. He was *not at home.*

"Why would I want to come and see that old dog anyway?" Ewatt boomed, clapping the butler on the shoulder so hard that the bony man's knees dipped and quivered, and he nearly fell. "I spy a far more enticing prospect. There you are! My good Lady Cornbrook! And what a vision you are. I fear I should not have partaken of dessert earlier for now I am quite overwhelmed with the sensation of sweetness."

"Mr Carter-Hall." She waved a gloved hand at him merrily. They had previously been introduced at the dinner Hugo had held for her arrival, and she knew him to be the local banker and all-round successful businessman. He had chattered to her most amiably that night.

"Call me Ewatt," he said, taking two strides across the terrace towards her.

"How frightfully modern, and I shall do no such thing," she said.

"But then I cannot call you Cordelia," he protested. He planted himself opposite to her, and bowed low.

"No, you may not. But do sit." She nodded at the spare ironwork chair. "I can ring for tea."

"You can ask for wine," he said. "I know Hugo has an immense cellar and this is my chance to sample some of the stuff he so jealously guards."

"I can hardly offer my host's goods to all and sundry. He will be annoyed with me."

"I am not all and sundry. And anyway, I shall defend

you with my life," Carter-Hall promised, sweeping his coat-tails up as he took a seat, his pudgy legs splayed apart and his eyes twinkling.

"I need no defending," she countered.

"Ah, and now who is being frightfully modern? Tell me, Lady Cornbrook, do you ride?"

"I do." She looked at his stocky frame with some doubt. "But do you?"

He roared with laughter at her open insinuation, and leaped suddenly to his feet. "Let us go!"

"You have barely sat down."

"I am a man of action," he declared, "though I see from your face that you are sceptical and need proof. Let not my rotundity deceive you. It is merely the unfortunate cut of my jacket, I promise. Come! My horse has just been taken around to the stables; and I am sure that Hugo will allow you the pick of his."

"There is a mare that he has apportioned for my use while I stay," she said. The banker's energy was infectious, and she stood up with a sense of excitement in her belly. "But you must excuse me while I change. You may as well be seated again, for this is not a swift process."

"Wine, then! And I shall see you in the stables anon."
He grinned, his bristling moustache spreading wide over
his face. She read all manner of intentions in his joviality,
and knew that not all of them were decent.

She remembered the elegant, giggling wife that he had
also brought to the dinner, but pushed the memory aside.
She was only going for a ride, and what harm could a
well-bred widow and a respectably married man really get
up to?

* * *

Within an hour, they were trotting briskly down a track
that ran in a straight, flat line between fields of ripening
crops. The harvest was being gathered in, and the farmland
was a patchwork of activity. They would pass one field
where every member of the farmer's family was engaged
there in tasks from reaping to gleaning, and the next field
would be bare, and the next one again full of golden corn
or wheat awaiting attention.

At first they spoke of local matters; how every inch of
Britain was coming under the creeping thrall of the railways,

as the tracks spread like tendrils into town and country. Carter-Hall told her of a suspension bridge, not too distant at Great Yarmouth on the coast, which had collapsed but three months past.

"Seventy-nine souls were lost," he said. "And a deal of money more, too."

"How awful. Are you a railway investor, sir?" she asked. She had taken shares in a number of companies, and was pleased with the results. She pulled the chestnut mare to a more sedate walk, and let her cool down. Carter-Hall rode his dark horse in an enthusiastic circle around them, twice, before matching her pace and coming alongside her.

"No, such mania is not for me," he said. "I will confess I was tempted but on both a personal and a professional level, I considered it initially a risk and then ... oh, well, my business has been leading in other directions. Ah! It is a dull thing, being in banking, and if I were to tell you more, you'd fall from your horse in a catatonic state. This is why I ride, Lady Cornbrook, for if I did not, I should one day be discovered at my desk quite melted away, nothing remaining of me but an insensible blob of jelly, dissolved into inert matter by the sheer tedium of working with numbers."

She laughed. "You are remarkably good with words for someone whose vocation is numerical," she said. "Are you following the right profession?"

"The tasks may be tedious but the rewards are potentially great," he said, and kicked at his mount's flanks. "Enough dull talk. Let us canter. Follow me!"

He led her off the track onto a broad green meadow and she fell easily into her mare's rocking rhythm, the broad side saddle comfortable. Cantering was certainly a more pleasurable experience than the harsh thump-thump of trotting, and she was grinning as they pulled up at the far side of the meadow. Carter-Hall dismounted. *He was not as athletic as he would lead her to believe,* she thought as he landed with a heavy thump, stifling a groan as his knees clicked audibly. She had leaped down with rather more grace before he was able to offer to assist her. Seeing her independence, he simply smiled and winked cheekily.

"Very good, my lady," he intoned like a spurned butler.

She allowed him to tend to the horses. She took a few steps back, retreating to the shade of a tree while he loosened their girths and led them to a trough in the corner of the field. It was only a quarter full, but it would not have been good for the hot animals to have drunk their fill too quickly. He seemed an expert horseman –if no gymnast – and was well used to knowing his beast's needs.

"And now for our refreshment," he said, pulling out a flattened flask from within his coat as he approached her. He held it out and she gratefully accepted. A nip of brandy was hardly thirst-quenching nor appropriate for mid-summer, but she didn't think he would be carrying a barrel of cider around with him.

It was fiery but energy-giving. She passed it back with a nod. "Thank you. Now, have you heard the biggest news of the day?"

His face became serious, the corners of his moustache drooping. "I believe you mean the murder of young Bains?"

"I do indeed."

"A sorry tale. And I heard that you were part of it," he said, tipping his head at an angle as he regarded her along his nose. His eyes had narrowed and she could not see much humour there. "It was a strange place for a woman such as yourself to be. People have been talking."

"*Such as myself*," she repeated. "Ah, as a widow I ought to be at home, closeted and praying? I did that for a number of years after the death of my husband. It has grown … trying. Now, things must change."

"Change they must," he said, with the hint of a laugh at last. "You ought to be married again, and therefore protected from the terrors of society."

"Married? Caged, you mean."

"Caged? Ah. You read novels, do you not?"

"I do," she said fiercely. "And it is as well that I do, for I had to instruct the silly shoemaker constable in his duties! It was I that insisted the doctor, and the coroner, were called to the scene."

Carter-Hall took the chance to change direction. "The coroner is now here," he said. "He arrived as I left my house. He is a fat and comfortable man, John Barron. I should imagine he rather resents being dragged away from his Cambridge dinners and forced to come out here. By the time the sun is risen again, he will have sworn in the jury, held the inquest, adjourned it for investigation, recalled it, discovered a verdict to send to the judge, and he'll be home for dinner that same night."

"Is he that good at his job?"

"No, but he's that quick, and what does it matter to

him, the death of a troublesome lad?"

"Did you know him, the dead man?" Cordelia asked. She began to repin her bonnet which had come loose. She did not want to tarry too long and let the horses become overly relaxed before they headed back to the manor.

"Oh, only by reputation, slightly, which is the way of things in small towns like this," Carter-Hall said, shrugging. He took another swig of the alcohol but Cordelia shook her head in refusal when he offered it to her. "After all, how would our paths ever cross? He was of a lowly station. He was an argumentative sort, from what I hear. You must ask Hugo, if you must, but it's not a fit topic for a lady, and a visiting one at that."

"Speaking of Hugo," she said, "we ought to get back. He will be returned now."

"I much prefer your company," he said, sidling closer. His hot breath tickled her neck. He was too near.

She stepped back very deliberately and continued to repin her hair and hat, using her elbows as a pointed defence. "How very kind of you to say so. Would you check the girth on my saddle, please?"

He let his gaze drop to her nipped-in waist, and she

frowned. Slowly she pulled one long hatpin free in a deliberate movement, and held it between them, keeping her eyes on his face.

He glanced at the sinister point, and laughed. "Lady Cornbrook, you are a singular woman with a definite streak of unconventional manners," he said. "But do you reject polite society as much as polite society rejects you?"

"Whatever do you mean?"

He regarded her levelly. "If you seek not to be married again – caged, as you say – then what will you do for company? By which I mean, male energy? By which I mean, of course, the tender embraces and fires of passion that once you knew in sacred matrimony that, once lit, can never be fully doused? I, too, am a married man, as you know. Yet I am prepared to extend my burning fires, my male energy if you will, to your very great benefit…"

Cordelia took a moment to unpick what he was proposing, then threw back her head and howled with laughter. She pushed the pin back into her bonnet, and let her guffaws recede to a more acceptable smile. Most men pursued her for her imagined money, but Carter-Hall was a different sort of man, and she had not expected anyone to want more of her than her marriageable portion, cash and stocks and status. She extended her hand and took the flask of brandy from him.

"I am honoured," she said. "You have brightened my day considerably. But…"

He knew the shape of the rejection. "I understand," he said, with placid acceptance. "It is not to be undertaken … today. Tomorrow, who knows?" He recovered his flask, tucked it away, and turned to the horses.

She watched the slant of his shoulder as he went about his business, and felt a strange sadness wash over her. *Oh, what could have been! Not today, and not tomorrow*, she told herself. That was not a path she wished to walk. It was not a path she could tread part-way to see if she liked it; once set upon it, her ruin would be certain. She would have a life, still, but not one that she chose.

They rode back to the manor briskly, and Carter-Hall chattered lightly about the SS Great Britain's progress across the Atlantic Ocean, and other such current marvels.

In her head, she was now calling him Ewatt.

CHAPTER EIGHT

In spite of her predictions, there was no sign of Hugo Hawke's grand carriage when Carter-Hall and Cordelia returned to the manor. They trotted around the side of the house and into a fine cobbled stable-yard, where her own coachman, Geoffrey Bloor, was attending to her almost-comfortable travelling chariot. More specifically, he was supervising the boy, Stanley Ashdown, while Stanley knelt in his shirt-sleeves, repainting the Cornbrook crest on the door of the coach.

Stanley didn't look up at her directly. She could not remember the youth ever making eye contact with her. Surely he would explode if such a transgression accidentally occurred. He could barely get a sentence past his lips when in her presence, and he'd been in her service since the age of fourteen; a good seven years, now. He had followed her from her childhood home where he'd worked for her father, and stayed with her. He was as awkward and gangly as ever he had been. She wondered at what age he'd grow into his elbows-and-knees frame. It didn't look likely to be any time soon.

Unlike Stanley's painful shyness, Geoffrey had no such reticence. He was a large, heavy-set man of darkness and muscle with a street-smart mouth and a well-stocked sword case on the back of the coach. He made the bare minimum of obsequiences to Cordelia, and turned his assessment, quite boldly, to Ewatt Carter-Hall.

It was almost as if he expected to be introduced to Ewatt, which simply wouldn't do. Cordelia sighed at Geoffrey's manners, and did the most effective thing, which was to ignore him. She frequently chose the easiest path when dealing with Geoffrey; a simple denial of his rudeness. She urged her mare forward and this time made use of the block to dismount. Still standing atop the mounting block, she turned to Carter-Hall and looked at him over the top of her mare's saddle.

"Thank you, sir, for a wonderful time," she said. Out of the corner of her eye she noticed Ruby and Mrs

Unsworth, her surly cook, approach from a back kitchen door. Now she was being watched by all the members of her retinue – Geoffrey, Stanley, Ruby and Mrs Unsworth – and she rather wished they would all go away.

And yet, for what purpose did she want privacy with this man? She had already established – to him, and to herself – that there was to be no impropriety here.

Still, it was nice to have the chance. She had enjoyed being admired and propositioned.

"The pleasure was all mine," Carter-Hall purred. He sat comfortably in his saddle, his stocky frame solid and reassuring in the way that he settled there. He might have had the hint of ungainliness about him when on his own feet, but he was an appealing figure when mounted. She tried not to look at his breeches. "You were a magnificent rider and I thoroughly enjoyed watching the manner in which you handled your horse."

The way his voice rumbled, with his moustache twitching and his eyebrows jerking upwards, made it sound as if they had been having criminal conversation together in the hedgerow, and Cordelia prayed fervently that she was wearing enough face powder to hide any betraying blushes on her cheeks. "I thank you, sir," she said.

"And I want to apologise, once more, if my bumbling country ways did in any way overstep any bounds or limits."

That was exactly what she did not want any of her servants to hear. *Go away*, she thought crossly. She kept on smiling as she said, brightly, "You have been the very model of propriety and honour, sir." *Now go home.*

"Then you would not object to me … taking you … again?" he said, and his eyes did not leave hers.

She heard the silly Ruby giggle at his phrase and she knew, then, that he had said it deliberately. *The cad.* "I am tired," she said. "I must rest. Good day."

It didn't answer his question but anyone of any decency knew when to stop pursuing the matter, and Carter-Hall withdrew, with a tip of his hat and a broad smile to Geoffrey, who growled at him as he trotted out of the stable yard.

Ruby could not suppress her giggles. Cordelia made her way down the stone steps and gathered up her mare's reins, just as she heard Ruby speak loudly to Mrs Unsworth.

"What manner of *riding* do you imagine has been going on twixt them?"

Geoffrey's growl turned to a snarl, and Mrs Unsworth glared at the maid. Without a word, the flabby cook turned on her heel and stamped heavily back into the house, slamming the door. She made it plain she wanted no part in it.

The coachman was another matter. "Geoffrey," Cordelia said, putting herself between the maid and the coachman. She held out the mare's reins. "Might you see to my horse? She has been ridden hard. Thank you."

He took the leather straps in his wide, calloused hand, but did not move to lead her away. Due to the heat, he was not wearing his usual long, dark overcoat. Under the summer sun, he was stripped right down to nothing more than black flannel trousers, a white collarless shirt with a white vest underneath, a faded black waistcoat, and a black jacket of an older style that had once been formalwear for a man more well-to-do than Geoffrey ever was. He had a dark grey kerchief knotted around his neck, and a tweed cap on his head. This was almost shocking undress for Geoffrey. And yet not a hint of sweat showed on his swarthy face. He stared past Cordelia, directly at the maid, and said in a slow grunt of menace, "You will mind your manners, Miss Ruby."

"Geoffrey, thank you," Cordelia said. "Enough. The mare? I shall see to my household discipline *with my own maid* as I see fit."

He turned his dark gaze on her. "As you wish, my lady," he said, in a dispassionate tone, lacking the threat he had injected into his words to Ruby. He clicked his tongue and took the mare forwards, walking in an unnecessarily large circle around the yard to change direction, so that his path went directly by Ruby. Cordelia did not hear what he muttered to her as he passed, but she could tell from the sudden look of defiance mingled with shock on the young woman's face that it was something terrifying.

Cordelia paused. What was it about her staff? At home, in her rambling large house, they all rubbed along without tension or distraction, or at least, so it had always seemed to Cordelia. Now they were abroad, travelling in the countryside, and it was as if rebellion fermented in every breast. That said, in her house, there were many more members of staff and they all had their allotted tasks and places. Travel threw all that into disarray. Even the very manner of travelling put Cordelia in closer and more constant contact with Ruby, trapped as they both were within the plush travelling chariot. Mrs Unsworth had also shared the inside space, though she had spoken not two words together for all the hours they had spent on the road.

Mrs Unsworth, of course, had her own counsel to keep and Cordelia was content to leave her alone.

Ruby was fast revealing herself to be an outspoken coquette with little check upon her tongue or manners. Geoffrey – ah, well, he had been in her service as long as anyone, and had been her late husband's man before, too, for many more years. So Geoffrey could be allowed a little leeway, perhaps.

But her maid was her own, she reminded herself. *She was not Geoffrey's concern at all.*

Geoffrey had tethered the mare to a post and was stripping her of the leather tack, now white-flecked with drying foam. He called Stanley over to leave his painting, and to come and groom the horse with a curry comb. The youth dashed over, head dipping and twisting as he scampered.

Cordelia was not going to reprimand Ruby out in the yard. She composed her face into what she hoped was a stern expression but as she approached the waiting maid, Ruby was smiling.

"Did you enjoy your ride, my lady?" she asked.

Cordelia stared, searching for a hint of insubordination and intentional double-meaning. Ruby's eyes were wide. Her hangover seemed to have been finally shaken off.

"I did," she replied stiffly. "I need to speak with you inside. And there is a soiree this evening; is my duck-egg blue gown prepared?"

"It will be directly, my lady. Who is to be present?"

"Hugo is inviting a handful of local worthies."

"Including that man? The big banker chap you were just riding with? My lady, in case you were not aware..." Ruby stammered to a stop, and to Cordelia's wonder, she was blushing.

Astonished, Cordelia urged her to finish. "You may speak freely," she said, hoping she would not regret that statement.

"My lady, I do not know you fully, and hope I do not overstep my place, and indeed I think I already have, but I speak only out of love and protection and ... my own experience," Ruby said, fixing her eyes on the floor, an entirely unexpected embarrassment settling on her. "You might have moved in carefully sheltered circles. Most ladies have. I had a previous mistress who ... well, she fainted the first day she saw a stallion, my lady. A stallion in his, ah, entirety. As it were. What I am trying to say, my lady, is that the intentions of that gentleman are not, to my mind, entirely honourable. The way he looks, and acts, his body and his hands ... tell a tale, my lady, that I can read. You must avoid him."

Cordelia's growing smile became a grin. *Wonderful child.* "Thank you, Ruby. I appreciate your candour and I shall not ask how you come by such particular knowledge. Suffice it to say that his intentions did become clear to me, but I was able to steer him into more reasonable waters."

"So he did not–"

"He was rebuffed," Cordelia said firmly. "Thank you. Now, let us go in and see to this dress. I will instruct you."

Ruby turned and went into the house but Geoffrey spoke as Cordelia made to follow.

"My lady," he called. "Do not fear. That man shall never bother you again, and I shall see to it myself."

She whirled around. "Geoffrey – no!"

"But you must have satisfaction."

"Under no circumstances are you to challenge Mr Carter-Hall to a duel," she said sharply.

Geoffrey laughed without humour. "Oh, not at all." He spread his thick, dirt-grained hands wide in the air. "Do I look like a duelling man to you, my lady?" he said.

He looked more likely to bite someone's ear off in an inn. "Ah – no. Simply … no," she snapped. "No, to *everything.*" She stalked off after Ruby, foreboding in her heart.

CHAPTER NINE

Ruby did her limited, untrained best in attending to Cordelia's eveningwear but both women knew that the current fashion for exposed, narrow and sloping shoulders did not favour Cordelia's athletic build. Still, Cordelia liked the colour of her chosen gown. It was restrained enough to be acceptable for a widowed woman, but a welcome relief from the months of mourning and half-mourning she had had to endure. Since that time, she had shied away from ever having black and grey in her wardrobe. The pale grey-blue of her gown was as close to a dull colour as she would get.

Full, flouncy lace sleeves hid her solid upper arms and she pulled a light, sheer shawl around her shoulders. Ruby had checked her gloves and satin shoes, and done wonders to tame her usually wayward hair into artful ringlets around her head, with a bun skewered tightly at the back. Whatever skills Ruby lacked in other areas, she was a surprisingly good dresser of hair.

Once she was ready, she waited in the outer room of the suite that she had been given for her visit while Ruby passed a message via circuitous means to the master of the house. It was warmer here than the unheated bedroom. She did not sit. Her layers of stiffened petticoats made her gown a perfect shape – at least for the moment – and she did not want to crumple Ruby's careful work. She paced up and down the Chinese-pattern carpet, weaving her way around the various tables that were scattered about the place, and wondered how the investigation into the death of Thomas Bains was progressing. She hoped that she might press some information out of the other guests that evening.

There was a sharp knock and the door was flung open before she could call out; but after all, this was Hugo's house. He burst into the room, all energy and dashing white teeth. He wore a dark blue dress coat with gleaming golden buttons, so nipped in to show his slender waist that his broad chest was almost that of a pugilist. His narrow, fitted trousers were of a fine black cashmere. Every inch of him, from his smart dress shoes to his silk top hat, was carefully calculated to demonstrate his good taste. He grinned, let his eyes sweep up and down her body, and then he bowed extravagantly. He was around Cordelia's age but his sandy hair was thick and luxurious, both on his head and his sideburns.

He was to propose marriage again, she assumed.

"My dearest Cordelia, you are a vision," he declared. "Now, I have invited but a handful of the very best people locally. And I have pressed a brilliant young pianist, name of Arthur something-or-other, to come out from Cambridge and delight us with some stirring pieces. It shall be a most select evening. Are you ready?"

"Of course." Whatever the unpleasant contracts that now bound them together, he was still a pleasing man and good company. She took his arm and they sailed down the wide stairs to meet the small, exclusive crowd.

* * *

She recognised most of the gathering from the dinner that Hugo had hosted previously. She nodded and smiled and let Hugo parade around, re-introducing her to this person and that. There was a tiny woman with no remarkable features whatsoever who was, apparently, a wealthy patroness of many charities and general philanthropist. There were a few interchangeable young bucks who stood around in a gang, all hanging on Hugo's every word. She greeted Ewatt Carter-Hall carefully, but he acted as if they had been brought up together in the same house, and cheerfully introduced her to his wife, Freda, a beautiful young woman with a vacant air who blinked and stared and simpered and was immediately distracted by a butterfly that had flown in through the open windows.

A matronly woman leaned forward, and said to the small group, "What of the dreadful business in town this morning! Have you heard?"

Her question was addressed to their little gathering of five, but Hugo rolled his eyes and pulled his arm free from Cordelia. "Do excuse me," he murmured, and abandoned her. He wandered off to join another small knot of people. In all, there were around two dozen present, all done up in their provincial best. The hall was decorated in the Regency style, yet it still retained a glamour even if it was not quite a la mode. The dark red walls were oppressive in the daytime, but at night, lit by the great cut-glass chandelier and many candles and lamps, it was a sparkling palace. The ornately carved frames of the huge paintings caught the light at odd, new angles and everything seemed slightly larger.

She watched Hugo go. She didn't mind that he'd left her; he'd be back. He had a mission, of course. She turned her attention back to the people nearest to her. Everyone was now talking of the murder, though no one really knew anything definite.

"Didn't the young man work here?" someone else said.

"I had heard so myself," Cordelia said. "What did he do?"

The other guests shook their heads, murmuring. "He was a servant," said one, their tone conveying their disbelief that they should be expected to know anything about what their staff actually did.

Now the attention was more fully focussed on Cordelia. The matronly woman assessed her curiously. "And how many years is it since the sad demise of your husband?" she asked.

"Five." She had been twenty-eight. "We had been married less than a year," she added, and was rewarded with the usual, predictable intake of breath.

"How perfectly tragic!" said one, a look on her face that actually said, "how perfectly thrilling!"

Certainly, the marriage had been tragic, though she wasn't so sure if she could honestly say that about his death. She bit her tongue, and smiled politely. She was about to ask more about Thomas Bains, in the hope that someone would know something, but she was interrupted by the matron once more.

"And at last you are re-entering society," she said, and shot a long and meaningful glance at Hugo Hawke's back.

"He had been urging me to visit for some time," Cordelia said. "I was becoming improper in my constant refusal. And naturally, as he is the trustee of my late husband's estates…"

The matron raised an eyebrow as if Cordelia was obscuring her true intentions. It was true that Hugo had been pursuing her assiduously, and it suddenly struck Cordelia as amusing. She had not expected to get married at all, so her late wedding to Lord Cornbrook had been a surprise to all. And her experiences should have put her firmly into the camp of eternal widowhood. Yet today, she had been impolitely propositioned by Carter-Hall, and Hugo Hawke himself was now watching her from across the room, and stroking his moustache rhythmically. For Cordelia, the clock was ticking in many ways. They had not yet "discussed the delicate matter" but his wishes were perfectly clear: marriage.

"It is certainly indelicate to remain in grieving for too long a time," the matron said. "A woman alone is an unprotected thing and prey to all manner of predators."

A woman with any kind of fortune is definitely prey, thought Cordelia. She smiled once more at the matron and excused herself from the discussion. Her retreat was too abrupt and hasty, and she could see the looks that passed between them as she made her way towards the piano, but she did not care. Her happiness did not depend on the approval – or not – of some provincial tittle-tattlers. Not any longer, so she vowed.

She had intended to place herself near to the talented pianist and simply enjoy the music for a time, but she was waylaid when she was only halfway there by the eager figure of Hugo Hawke once more. He was holding two glasses of temptingly sparkling champagne and he pressed her to accept one.

"Cordelia," he said. "I must apologise for abandoning you to those harpies. I saw Ewatt and had to catch him to arrange a card game later."

"Mixed?" she asked hopefully.

"Regretfully not," he said. "I know what a ferocious player you are, Cordelia, and I have no doubt you should bankrupt us all. But you would be the only lady, and we men get shockingly rowdy in our cups."

"You would be amazed how rowdy I can be," she said. *Or how rowdy I imagine I might be, given a chance.*

Instead of appalling him, it seemed to light a fire in his eyes. "No doubt," he said, licking his lower lips. "Now, I know you are interested in the literary arts. Have I shown you the Japanese manuscripts in my library?"

"No, I don't believe you have. That sounds fascinating."

"Would you like to step into the library with me?"

She knew, immediately, that the alcohol in his system was igniting the passion in his loins, and that he wanted to get her alone. She wondered if he even had any Japanese manuscripts. Anyway, did they not write on scrolls? She was unsure. Hugo's eyes were dark and hungry. If she were lucky, he intended to inflict upon her nothing more than an excited declaration of love and proposal of marriage. If she were unlucky, he would skip the words and proceed directly to the physical. Neither option was appealing at this moment. She wanted to put her decision off for as long as possible.

"Perhaps tomorrow," she said. "I would rather see them in daylight. The lamplight is not good for my aging eyes."

"Aging!" he spluttered, but she was slipping away as he protested, and she didn't look back though she heard him laugh. She felt bad for spurning him but it could never do. A drunken man was unpredictable.

Was she leading him on? She sighed, suddenly feeling crushed by the enormity of her impending decision. When the five years of grace were up, she would have to find somewhere to live. Her investments were making her a good income, but she had grown so attached to Clarfields. The expectation was that she would marry; and Hugo, the trustee, expected that she marry him.

She knew what she ought to do. And the second time around it should be easier. But it was not.

She wove her way through the large hall of the manor and out through a sun room onto the darkening terraces. Unescorted, unaccompanied, she knew that scandals could attach to a woman such as herself.

Maybe she should not have come. She should have remained at Clarfields, where she was secure, and had Hugo come to discuss her future there. By coming here, she was adrift and without all her comforts and familiar staff. Yet she could stay cooped up in her own house no longer. Her options for visiting others were limited; her family dead, and just the hint of scandal still attaching to her from her marriage. She could visit her late husband's distant relatives, but they were less appealing than her mad aunt in Yorkshire.

The cool air ruffled her ringlets, and she stood by a stone urn, her hand resting on the top as she gazed out into the layers of grey and shadow that made up the garden at night. The moon was only a slip of a crescent, and half-hidden behind scudding clouds.

She was startled when she heard a gentle footstep behind her, but it was Hugo once more, this time clutching a whole bottle of champagne, freshly opened, wispy pale clouds still clinging to the glass. "Would you care for a drop more?" he asked.

"You will think me a frightful lush," she said as she proffered her glass.

He shrugged. "I admire a woman of appetite," he said meaningfully. "What a peaceful night. Warm, too."

"It is. And you have a beautiful house." *Houses*, she added in her head. *You have what is mine. Mine! Clarfields.*

"Thank you. Cordelia, if I may be so bold to speak freely?"

Her heart sank but she inclined her head. This was it. "Of course."

"I am a man of action. I don't have the flowery words or gift of rhetoric like some men. You've spoken with Ewatt. I can't charm a woman like he can. I like drinking and riding and travel and playing cards and laughing very loudly. I like my house and my life and my friends. I am blessed. Blessed in all things but one…"

She could not help but let her eyes flick over his body, downwards, and she was delighted to see that he darkened slightly, a blush visible even in the dusk, when he realised where she was looking. "Madam!" he spluttered, suddenly taken aback.

She feigned innocence. "Go on," she murmured sweetly.

"I mean to say, that is, that I have enjoyed your company these past few days."

"And I yours." *To a point.* He was amusing enough. She fell silent as he searched for words.

"And … that I am trying not to be such a hothead," he said in a rush. "So, please, do stay in my house for as long as you please, if you are comfortable here. I know we have another matter to discuss… but all in good time."

That was it? She was almost disappointed, though she had not been looking forward to the conversation. She smiled with genuine warmth. "Thank you, Hugo," she said, boldly using his first name. "I have no doubt that everything will resolve to our mutual benefit." She meant only to speak politely but it sounded, once uttered, like an acceptance.

And it triggered him to move in a little closer and she wondered, suddenly, if she had misjudged the whole thing and he was, indeed, about to leap upon her bodily. But at the same instant, their attention was jointly caught by a rustling in the buddleia and rhododendron bushes that lined the edge of the lawn below.

She dropped her voice. "What was that?"

He moved to her side but in a pleasingly protective way. She liked the smell of his cologne. "I would not be afraid of the murderer," he murmured. "Not here. It is far more likely to be one of our resident hedgehogs."

She hadn't even thought of the possibility of a murderer on the prowl until he said that. She shook her head. "Oh, hedgehogs? I would like to see."

He took her empty glass and placed it on the low wall with his own, and the bottle. Together, they hunched over and stalked silently down the steps, the wine in their blood making them giggle and exaggerate their movements. Her thin satin pumps were no protection against the stray stones on the path and she quickly moved onto the neatly trimmed lawn.

As they drew nearer to the looming black bush, Hugo put out a hand and pulled her back, by the elbow. It startled Cordelia and made her squeal, and the leaves suddenly shook hard, with an answering squeal from deep within the foliage.

Cordelia took two paces back, quickly, cannoning into the solid body of Hugo who was instinctively coming forwards; she cried out, "Oh!" as two figures stumbled out of the bushes. Just as quickly, another large dark figure emerged from a path that went between the house and the bushes, and leaped between them all, arms outstretched, as if to protect Cordelia from the two figures that had been lingering.

There was confusion.

"Mistress!"

"Ruby!"

And the cloaked man in the hat, standing in the centre of them, growled out, "Ruby, you harlot – and who is that you are with? Bert the footman?"

Hugo pushed himself in front of Cordelia, but he seemed confused as to who he ought to be defending her from. He made a circle with his hands, as if to take them all on in a boxing match. He did look dashing. Cordelia giggled.

She stepped forward and pulled his upraised fists down, and spoke to the cloaked man. "Oh, Geoffrey. Look at you. What are you doing there?"

"I was looking for this errant minx," he said defensively, pointing at the white-clad and now-shivering maid. Even in the half-light of the gathering night, she could see that Ruby was in some disarray.

Cordelia sighed. "Ruby, get inside. Go up to my rooms, now."

There was no argument, and the maid bolted for a back door. The footman, likewise dishevelled, stood stock still for a moment, but Geoffrey grunted and he, too, ran, straight across the lawn and towards the stables.

"What larks," Hugo said, gathering his wits. "Bert! I didn't know he had it in him. Remind me to check the state of his livery tomorrow. Cordelia, your maid is a live one, is she not?"

"She is, indeed. And I shall see to her directly." She tried to throw a stern glance at Geoffrey but he tipped his head up so that she faced only his jutting chin, his features in darkness.

"Geoffrey, you may retire."

"As you wish." He paused for a moment. *If he was waiting for thanks,* Cordelia thought, *he shall wait for eternity. It is not that I am not grateful, but this was not his place.*

The moment stretched out, until Hugo coughed, and finally Geoffrey tipped his cloth cap with a perfunctory flick of his wrist, and withdrew into the shadows once more.

"It is good that he keeps an eye on the maid," Hugo remarked as he led Cordelia back up onto the terrace where they rescued their wine and poured more.

Cordelia didn't reply. *It was a wonder that Ruby wasn't with child several times over. A wonder? A blessing. Or a curse.*

And it was a wonder, indeed, that Geoffrey was keeping an eye on her.

If it was, indeed, Ruby that he was so assiduously watching.

CHAPTER TEN

Ruby and Cordelia drove in the freshly-painted carriage to town the following morning. The journey was short and silent, with Ruby staring at the floor and Cordelia leafing through a novel that was packed, cover to cover, with rich colonels and trembling maidens. It was the sort of entirely unsuitable novel she had hoped to confiscate from her servants, but when none had obliged – among them all, only Stanley read books, and the boy favoured stern religious tracts and The Bible – she had had to purchase the books herself from a club.

They came to a halt. Cordelia was ready with her bonnet and gloves, her hand on the side of the window, but there was a longer than usual delay before Geoffrey opened the coach door.

"My lady," he said, his bulk filling the doorway, "it's

rather busy."

She put a gloved hand on his shoulder and peeked past him at the general bustle in the town. "It's hardly Oxford Street," she chided him. "And I have a need for dark blue ribbons. Come, now. Don't fuss. Take the horses to the inn. Ruby and I will explore the market, and then we shall dine at the inn. If you could go in and secure a private room for us, that would be marvellous." Her hand tapped him encouragingly until he moved out of the way.

There was no difference between road and walkway in this country town. The lady and her maid inched their way along, and it was a small mercy that the way was dry, mostly. Only the spots where horses were standing had to be avoided; not so much for the emissions of the horses, but the spilling of large quantities of water made the ground muddy and churned.

"He does take some liberties," Cordelia muttered to herself, pulling a strand of black cotton from her white glove. It had come loose from Geoffrey's many garments.

Ruby was still alongside, wearing her usual pale gown with a pretty but worn yellow embroidered shawl around her. "It is only that he cares for you, my lady, and better that than an indifferent servant."

I wonder which you are, Cordelia thought. *I think you will be whatever suits you at the time.* "Yes, you are right, my dear."

There was nothing more to say. Cordelia had spoken very sharply to Ruby in the morning. She had hoped to discipline her the previous evening, soon after her transgression in the bushes with the footman, but Ruby had been in hiding and for a while Cordelia assumed she had run away. However, in the morning she had emerged from the small anteroom where she had her bed, as if she had been there all night, and set about laying out Cordelia's toilette as normal.

It wasn't so much the shenanigans with the young man, Cordelia thought. She had explained as much to Ruby. It was the embarrassing lack of discretion that was the problem.

* * *

Cordelia bought ribbons, a bonnet and ordered some ham to be delivered to Hugo's kitchens. Likewise, the haberdashery would be taken by a boy to the house, leaving Ruby and Cordelia free to wander unencumbered. They were surprised to see Geoffrey standing in the place they had left him, close to the town square.

"What is the matter? Why are you not at the inn?" Cordelia demanded.

Geoffrey nodded his head in the closest he could get to a deferential greeting. "'Tis too busy, my lady. There's not a space in the stable yard nor a room to be got within. The coroner is arrived and it seems he has sworn in his jury. Not the jury for trial though; I don't rightly understand what they are saying. But I do know that the sheriff is on his way, and a room set aside for him. There are even a few newspapermen come from Cambridge but they are young bucks; reckon there is no point sending their important men as it's not so big a story, excepting that it was the landlady as did it."

"And therein lies the injustice," Cordelia said, staring past Geoffrey at the wide, red-brick coaching inn. There were crowds on the steps, pushing past one another but no one was able to enter. "And I ought to lay it bare for the coroner. Poor Mrs Hurrell." She took a step towards the inn but stopped. She could see, even without Ruby's sigh and Geoffrey's grunt, that she was not going to gain admittance to the place.

"I shall drive you back to the house," Geoffrey said. "My lady."

"No." She whirled around and stepped back up into the carriage, seizing the chance to do so unassisted by Geoffrey. "I shall wait here. I am hungry. So, too, must you be, and Ruby also. If there are no rooms available for me within, then I shall remain on my own property – here. Geoffrey, you go into the back rooms of the inn, where men of your sort assemble, and buy some food that might be easily carried. Ruby, you can seek out some drinks. Here." She pulled out some coin from her purse and handed it to the two startled servants.

"But where will you eat?" Ruby asked.

Cordelia looked around pointedly. The street was a place of meals as much as it was a place of commerce, conversation and entertainments. It was a fact that many people crowded into small rooms with no means of cooking, even here in a country town. It was the way of life, especially in London and cities, and common enough in smaller places. A working man could buy his coffee for breakfast on the way to work, buy a bread roll for a midday meal if he were lucky, and buy a pie for the evening. The air was thick with the smell of food.

There weren't any other fine ladies preparing to make a picnic of it in their carriages, however.

"I am a widow," she said to the world at large. "Who really cares what I do? Ruby, Geoffrey; go to it."

* * *

Cordelia was left alone for a long time. She read her book for a little while, before sitting back on the cushions, with the door pulled closed, thinking. Stanley sat atop the carriage, silently watching. *He would have been little use if someone tried to rob me*, she thought. She drew her purse a little closer to her hip, placing it on the seat by her side, so that her hand could grab a sharp tortoiseshell comb easily. *One jab of that into someone's eyes*, she thought, *would be pleasingly effective.*

She tried not to long for such an event to happen. For something – anything – to shake her out of her ennui. Oh, what fancies did a bored mind entertain! She rested her head back against the seat and sighed. *The Devil really did make work for idle hands,* she reflected. Here she was, imagining stabbing a footpad, and quite relishing the idea.

But if she were to avoid boredom and the Devil's entreaties to mindless violence, what work could she usefully do? Her books were a dismal failure. Her investments were mostly handled by her agent in London. She had to think of moving out of her house and taking rooms somewhere – a seaside town, perhaps. She could have an affair with Ewatt. He seemed keen, though it would ruin her utterly. Or she could marry Hugo; she barely knew him but he seemed joyful and energetic.

Try as she might, every time she bent her thoughts to Hugo Hawke, they skittered away to something else. It was as if her mind didn't want him in there.

I just don't know him well enough, yet, she told herself.

She pulled out her notebook and glanced at her list of projects. There was so much she wanted to learn, to know, to see . . . but without a reason for that, it seemed so pointless.

"My lady!" Ruby was back, carrying two glasses and a bottle on a tray. Cordelia jumped and pushed her notebook away. "They were for giving me beer," Ruby was saying apologetically. "I would have been back sooner but I had to make quite a fuss to get them to serve me wine instead."

"Beer would have been fine," Cordelia said. "I've never had beer. I'm told it's an acquired taste."

"You acquire it if you've no other choice," Ruby said. "It is not for you, my lady."

Soon after, Geoffrey returned, his dour face even more drawn into a scowl than usual. "They did not understand what I was asking for," he muttered. "I could not serve you Mystery Pie. This took some getting." He had three pewter plates in his two hands, the middle plate precariously overlapping to balance between the others. There was a suet pudding on each, with rich dark gravy oozing out. "This is hardly appropriate for a woman of your station," he said as Ruby took a plate. She wiped the edge all the way around with her handkerchief before she passed it to Cordelia.

"It is perfectly delightful," she replied. "And most exciting."

Geoffrey, now with one hand free, tossed a coin up to Stanley. "Go find a pie, boy." The carriage rocked as the lad jumped down. Geoffrey was about to climb up into his place but Cordelia stopped him.

"What news from within?" she asked. "Regarding the murder, I mean."

Geoffrey snorted. "They say that the one who was killed, that Thomas, was an argumentative sort, who would spend a night telling you the sky was pink if the fancy took him. He had very little learning and what he did have, he did not use. He is the general topic of gossip, but I can't say as anyone really misses him."

Cordelia had not realised that Stanley was still nearby until he stammered out, "Yet he too … as are we all … was a ch-child of God."

"Not by any account," Geoffrey retorted. "He were a poor church-goer and a poorer worker. Go, get your food, boy. No sermonising here."

Stanley scampered off. Geoffrey disappeared onto the seat up top, and Ruby pulled the carriage door closed so that the general public would not witness the shameful lack of standards currently being demonstrated.

"And what gossip have you heard, girl?" Cordelia said to Ruby. The inn had provided eating irons in the shape of a spoon for each, and it was a new skill to attack the soft suet pastry with any decorum. She kept her eyes on her food and waited for Ruby to begin to speak.

She could tell that Ruby was reluctant to open up, as she was still smarting from the morning's dressing-down. But she had information too delicious to keep to herself, and eventually she broke. The bribery of a good, hot pie could do wonders.

"Well, my lady, I know that you pay no heed to the notion that it was Mrs Hurrell, the landlady, as did the deed."

"Indeed, I think it most improbable."

"The town, though, thinks otherwise. Most are set upon her as the perpetrator. She is not local, you know. That counts for an awful lot."

Cordelia remembered back to the scene in the cottage. "She had been here eight years," she said. "And where did she live before?"

"London, where they say that she had a house that was … disorderly. Ah, um… I don't rightly know how to explain this to you."

Of course. London ways. It came back to her. "I know exactly what you mean. You have little need to be coy with me. I am not like that mistress of yours who could not cope with the sight of a stallion, nor am I innocent in the ways of the meaner streets of London. I was married to a man who ... So, she was a madam, this Mrs Hurrell, of a sort. But what did she do here? Her trade was otherwise, I am guessing?"

"There was no suggestion that she was anything other than a respectable landlady while she lived here."

"Well. Stanley would be pleased to remind us that we can all repent of our sins and be saved."

They fell silent for a respectful moment, and Cordelia took some wine. It was slightly watered down, but it was drinkable. She poured a scant half-glass for Ruby. She surmised the maid would have had a glass already, while inside the inn.

"And what of the victim himself?" Cordelia asked. "Tell me all. Did you hear the same information that Geoffrey had?"

"Yes. Though what is odd, my lady, is that they spoke of his words as being fighting words but he never laid a fist upon anyone. He has never, ever fought with anyone, as far as anyone can recollect. He had a perversely generous streak. Once, they said, he gave his coat to a beggar woman. They mocked him for his weakness, though if a minister of religion had done such a thing, would not people praise him?"

"That is true. Society does want people to act only as they are marked to act."

Ruby shrugged. "So, he was not a fighter, just a shouter. He argued with Mrs Hurrell. He argued with Ralph, the head gardener at the house – he argued a lot with him, about all manner of things, and did not work well there. He even argued, it is said, with the doctor."

"Now there is a man I cannot imagine arguing," Cordelia said. "He is altogether too in command of his emotions, his body, and his entire being. Have you ever seen a man so pressed in on himself?"

"He cuts a fine figure," Ruby said wistfully. "There is a man for whom tight breeches were designed."

"They said he was often to be seen performing callisthenics in the open fields," Cordelia said, lost in her own thoughts for a moment.

"They said all sorts," Ruby pointed out. "And then ... they laughed. Some of the folks in the inn do like the doctor; he attends to all people, if he can, even if they are poor, and he does not overcharge. But they laugh at him, also. And to my mind, that laughter, it has an edge. Like they do not quite trust him."

Cordelia was shocked. "Why would they distrust such a well-to-do trained man?"

Ruby sat back and a scornful look flitted over her face, her ripe lips curling just a little. "My lady, what reason have the poor to trust any man like that?"

CHAPTER ELEVEN

It was Cordelia's turn to sink into an almost-sullen silence as they drove back to Hugo's house. She pretended to read her book, but she was instead turning things over in her mind.

Why wouldn't the poor folk of the town trust a well-educated man? She probed at it, worried at it, looked it at from all angles. If someone was of a higher standing, and had an expansive education, of course you would trust them.

She asked herself who she trusted, but the first name that popped into her head was, curiously, Stanley Ashdown. *Why that name?* He was poor; a mere servant. She closed her book. The young man was taciturn, easily intimidated, and quite rigid with religious morals. He would attend Church every day if he had the time.

"Here we are, my lady."

"Oh! I hadn't even noticed we had stopped. Ah, thank you, Geoffrey. Ruby, I fancy I shall take a walk in the gardens. I have much on my mind. Will you see to the deliveries and ensure they have arrived from town?"

"My lady."

She passed her book and her purse to Ruby to convey into the house, but did not follow. She watched Geoffrey take the carriage and horses to the right, heading for the stables. She waited until she was alone, although the windows of the wide manor watched her still.

The weather was not as hot as it had been of late. After a few moments of contemplation, she made up her mind, and began to head around the left hand side of the house, heading towards the array of greenhouses and vegetable plots that she had spied hidden behind the house. This was an unexplored area for her.

All was quiet. She passed under a brick arch and entered a haven enclosed on all sides by tall walls. Only the vast size of the kitchen garden ensured that it still felt open rather than hemmed in. The paths were laid to gravel and bordered by low, well-clipped box.

She walked between glasshouses teeming with the

summer explosion of ripening soft fruits and delicate vegetables. At the end of the path stood a larger greenhouse, this one of white-painted wrought iron, and clearly the showpiece of the gardens. The doors stood open, letting the build-up of summer heat escape, and she could see tumbling arrays of colourful flowers on staggered staging within.

When she was ten feet from the greenhouse, a man suddenly rose to his feet from behind an enormous jungle of rhubarb. He was a weather-beaten man with skin like roughed-up wood, sinewy and bow-backed and bow-legged. He stared at her, then tugged off his hat and stared at the floor, the tips of his ears bright red. He did not speak.

"Good afternoon. Are you the head gardener, Goody? Ralph Goody?"

"Yes m'm," he mumbled. "Ralph Goody it is. Please forgive me. I had not been awarned of a visit."

"No, no, it was not planned. You may relax."

Ralph relaxed by staying entirely rigid and keeping his eyes on the floor.

She knew she wasn't going to unbend this old traditional servant by simply subjecting him to a barrage of questions. She glanced towards the greenhouse. "Please, though, I should be utterly delighted if you were able to spare a few moments to show me your wonderful flowers. It is one of my interests."

"Yes, m'm." He straightened slightly, as much as his sloping shoulders would allow, and tried to wipe his earth-caked hands on his green trousers. He stepped carefully, and when he reached the edge of the plot, he used a boot-scraper – one of many fixed at intervals around the garden – so that his muddy boots did not sully the gravel path.

He didn't look at her, but as soon as they were within the stuffy glasshouse, he became animated. *A man is a king in his own small realm*, she thought, as she walked alongside him and let him grow passionate about the camellias that ranged along the side, their pink heads nodding above them. He called them "tea flower" and pointed to their constant need for water. "Also, master has brought back orchids from his travels," Ralph went on, as they turned around at the far end of the greenhouse and began to walk back up the other side. He showed her the delicate and bizarre flowers Hugo had acquired on his travels. "Though I think he does not understand the craze for them that some men have."

"These are marvellous," she said. "You have worked so hard. And is that *Mirabilis jalapa*? There, the red and yellow blooms."

"The marvel of Peru," Ralph said, nodding. He began to talk to her as one who knew plants, and she was pleased.

"I believe you can use the flowers to dye sweets and jellies," she said. "I would like to try that. I am fascinated by the culinary arts."

"I can arrange to have some sent to the kitchen," he said. "It would be no trouble at all. Anything here in the garden is at your disposal, m'm."

"Thank you. I appreciate that." They stepped out into the cooler open air and she surveyed the vegetables. "You do work hard."

"Thank you, m'm. Been here since I were eight years old, and now I'm well into my fifth decade, somewhere, I think."

"Goodness me. And you manage all this alone?" she probed.

"No," he said, making a strange creaking noise that she

was slow to identify as a chuckle. "I do have a few boys to help me out."

"That murdered lad, Thomas Bains, was one, was he not?"

"On occasion but I had no truck with that one." He stiffened up.

She decided to tread carefully. She nodded towards a smaller greenhouse. "May I?"

"Of course." He led her into a room of glorious melons and exotic gourds, and she made appreciative noises.

When he was relaxing again, she said, "Thomas was argumentative, they say. I imagine he was a poor worker."

"Aye, oftentimes late, oftentimes lazy. He stole food, I am sure of it, also, and I brought it to the master's attention. He was not to be trusted."

"How very responsible of you! It must have been very difficult to work with one such as Thomas."

"Aye, so it was, m'm."

"It is the gossip of the town. And they say it was a woman, his landlady, that did the deed!" she prompted.

To her surprise, Ralph shook his head. He scratched his neck thoughtfully as he stared past Cordelia, out of the greenhouse and across his gardens. "Well, people do say all manner of things and I am but a poor gardener and it is not in me to have big thoughts. But I cannot see it, myself."

"She wasn't local…"

"Aye but nor is anybody if you go back far enough," he said. "Though a garden is where it all began. This is the only place we can truly be at home. No, as for Mrs Hurrell, she came from a bad place but she came away, and that is the thing, is it not? To leave and start anew. That's courage."

"London's not so bad," Cordelia said, smiling.

"I mean Eagle Street. She had a house there … oh, begging pardon, m'm…"

"It's perfectly all right," she reassured him. "I am aware of the nature of her business there."

"It was a respectable one, such as it can be, though, from what I did hear," he said. "A bad one but not as bad as some might be, is all." He trailed off and dropped his gaze, and she let him lead her out into the garden once more.

"Have you herbs here?" she asked.

"Aye, for the kitchen," he said, and took her closer to one of the back doors. That made sense; they would have to be accessible for the cook. "We have all the herbs and flavours that any cook might need."

"And plants for the sickroom also," she said, noting the feverfew and lavender. "I suppose that Mr Hawke had little cause to ever call the doctor, though."

"Oh, I doubt we should ever see the likes of him here. As a professional man, I mean. Who the master chooses to invite to his dinners, however, is his own business." Ralph's face was closing up once more.

"The doctor strikes me as an unusual man…"

"Aye." The single word was bitten off. He stared off past her again, pointedly looking towards the rhubarb patch.

She took the hint, and thanked him profusely for his time. She walked slowly back along the crunching gravel, her head now whirling with information. She had no confidence in the constable to get to the bottom of matters. Doctor Donald Arnall was intriguing her more and more.

Furthermore, the tour of the kitchen gardens had given her a new idea – a possible new outlet for her energy and time – which was making her quiver with its potential. She would not think of the ending of her time at Clarfields. She would think only of the future.

A trip to the Post Office was going to be essential. She felt dizzy with the excitement of being at the starting line of a new project, and smiled as she skipped up the steps to the house.

CHAPTER TWELVE

The afternoon was wearing on but Cordelia was keen to put things into motion. She hurriedly wrote her letters at her small travelling box, opened out on the table in the day room of her suite. The windows were open and the fire unlit, and the summer air flowed into the room. Ruby busied herself in the background, rustling through from the sitting room to the bedroom and back again, preparing a suitable outfit for Cordelia to wear on her walk into town. She refused any offers of company, and brushed aside Ruby's indignant protests.

"I shall be highly surprised to find I have any honour remaining that might be compromised," she told the maid as she swapped her shoes.

Ruby cocked her head and looked about to reply. Cordelia stopped her, rising to her feet and saying, firmly, "No."

"I didn't say—"

"You were about to. Has the ham arrived?"

"Yes, my lady, and Hugo's cook is arguing with Mrs Unsworth."

"I would doubt the sanity of anyone who did not argue with Mrs Unsworth," Cordelia said drily. "Now, I shall not be long." She tested the letters and found the ink was now quite dry, so she folded them and sealed the envelopes. "You may relax; attend to your Bible, or do some mending, perhaps."

She knew that it was not the sort of thing that Ruby would call "relaxing." With a merry wave, she left her maid to get up to whatever sneaky trysts she could manage, and headed along the road to town once more.

* * *

The Post Office occupied one half of a general store; the calmer, less crowded half, she discovered. In the shop side, people crowded around the counter, waiting as the shop keeper and his boy fetched their items and packed them, but the half containing the Post Office counter was devoid of people. The walls were a pleasant cream which showed the polished woodwork nicely. Behind the post office clerk were a range of shelves with a few items proudly displayed, unlike the general chaos of the shop part of the business.

The post office clerk was short and round, with bushy white whiskers. He smiled broadly and leaned forward as she approached, looking behind her for her companions. He had enough polite breeding to let only a sliver of surprise show on his face when he learned she was unaccompanied.

No doubt he thinks me the finer sort of jade, she thought, and almost giggled to herself.

"Good afternoon, sir. I wish to send two letters," she said, pulling them from her bag as she reached the counter.

"With pleasure, madam." He took them and studied the addresses. "London and ... where is this?"

"My estate in the county of Surrey," she said, and he took a pen to add the county name to the bottom of her envelope. The words stuck in her throat.

"Very good. One penny each, if you please."

"I still marvel that it costs the same for any distance," she said as she paid.

"Indeed, it is a wonder. And much work it has caused for me and my assistants; not that I am complaining, no, indeed!"

"Work?" She indicated the empty room.

"Oh, I take your meaning," he said. "But all my boys are out, meeting this stage or that train, with their letters and parcels and errands. Quite the rush we've had on, today, I must confess." He leaned his elbows on the counter and affected a confidential tone. "And folks I do not usually see here more than once in a month! And sending such a slew of letters! There must be something in the air."

He wasn't just gossiping, she realised. He was inviting her to partake of his gossip. Well, working in a communications office was perfect for a garrulous and inquisitive man such as he seemed to be. And what a refreshing change from earlier, when she had had to tease out scraps of information from Ralph Goody the gardener.

"Oh, really?" she replied, leaning forward slightly herself, and lowering her voice. She met his eyes and tried to sound coquettish.

"Now, you're not from round here…" he said.

Oh, so it was to be a trading of information, she thought. *It was his currency.* "I'm staying with Huge Hawke," she told him.

He nodded; he already knew. Everyone did.

She had to tell him more. "I have been widowed these five years past," she said. "And as such, my life is constrained and narrow. But dear Hugo was my late husband's trustee and he has been kind enough to invite me to stay so that I might see a little of society."

She dropped enough insinuation into her words to set the clerk's mind whirring away like a clockwork automaton. She smiled as if in perfect innocence as she conjured up the beginnings of a scandalous rumour for him. "I have lacked for all male company lately. Hugo is so very dear to me. And Mr Ewatt Carter-Hall, too, has been *most* attentive. I cannot express my gratitude enough for *his* ministrations!"

"Oh, yes," the clerk agreed, his eyes sparkling with rumour upon assumption upon simply more rumour. "Mr Carter-Hall has always been noted for his propensity to render assistance to the female sex. Indeed, he was one of the men with a curious number of letters to send today."

"Did he really?" she murmured. "I suppose he must have an awful lot of frightfully important work…"

"I rather think he must be planning a trip abroad," the clerk said. "Mind, he said nothing of it to me, directly. But when one works in an office such as this, one does become an uncommonly good reader of people."

Oh, are you? she thought, amused, but she let him continue in his self-importance. "For example," he said, his pudgy finger beating the points on the counter in rhythm to his words, "one of his letters was to a shipping company in London and another to a broker there. Furthermore, he had letters to France – one to an agent and one to a property company. There, you see! With those morsels of information, one can read all a man's intentions, can one not?"

"Quite," she said. "Quite so. And who else has been unusually active in here today?"

"There is a doctor in these parts…"

"Doctor Arnall. Yes, we met at a dinner." *And over a corpse,* she added silently.

"Doctor Donald Arnall," the clerk said. "Indeed. And he is not a local man, either. A strange one. He reads newspapers altogether with too much *intent*." A good man would not sully himself with politics, was the insinuation, one often expressed by the established churches.

"Where does he hail from?" she asked.

"Liverpool," the clerk said. "Though his voice is not as odd as the natives there. But it is Liverpool where all *his* letters were going!"

"That is not so very strange," Cordelia pointed out. "His family might well be there, and his friends remain there also."

"Indeed, it would have not been strange at all – if his letters had been going to friends and family!" the clerk declared with a flourish. "But no! Not a private house among the addresses. He wrote to hospitals – not one, but many! Prisons, also. What do you make of that?"

"Goodness." She had not expected to be surprised but she straightened up and stared in wonder. "I have no idea what to make of that. How curious. And he gave no intimation as to the contents?"

"None at all." The clerk shrugged. "I am not privy to the man's confidences. I rather doubt that anyone is."

"But he is married, is he not…"

"He is. Happily, so they say," the clerk added, as if warning her off.

She smiled. No doubt there would be some scurrilous rumours about to take wing now. "Thank you for seeing to my letters," she said, and gathered her shawl more tightly about her shoulders. "I must be returning."

* * *

She sorted through the new information in her head as she strolled back along the lonely road to Hugo's house. So, the doctor came from Liverpool – what had prompted him to write to hospitals and prisons there? And Ewatt, well, she could imagine that he did travel a lot. So his letters were not so strange at all. The clerk was finding gossip in the smallest of things.

A trip to Europe, though, she thought. *How exciting! I should travel. Maybe the loss of my house will be freeing for me.* Would Ewatt take his distractible wife? She had the attention span of a kitten, and the appealing looks of one, too. No doubt she was as distracting as she was easily distracted.

Perhaps, instead, Ewatt would leave her at home, and travel alone. Or, more thrillingly, with a mistress.

She was intrigued for a moment. What would that be

like? The offer was there from him. She could travel on the arm of a rich man, laughing and drinking their way through the respectable haunts of the continent, perhaps even pretending to be a married couple. It was often done so. She knew of society ladies who had fallen into such a life. Some had regretted it, but others professed not to. Many doors were closed to them, but perhaps that only meant that other doors were open to more exciting places.

Her words to Ruby earlier had been a lie. She had claimed she had no honour to lose. In truth, she knew that a fall from what unsteady grace she currently held would be catastrophic for one such as her. For Ewatt would tire of her; he would cast her off; and then, alone, she would truly be ruined.

There would be no more invitations to houses such as Hugo's, she reminded herself. He would not marry her. No one would.

She picked up her pace. She would now await the replies to her letters. One, she had sent to her house, informing them that she would be absent just a little while longer while matters were arranged.

The other was to her literary agent in London, and it

assured him of the details of her amazing new plan for success.

CHAPTER THIRTEEN

Hugo was pleased that Cordelia declared her intention to accept his offer of a longer stay. He assured her they would "settle the matter" soon. He also happily gave her directions to Ewatt's house, and advised her that Freda Carter-Hall was often "at home" and would likely be grateful for a visit.

"I fear she misses the whirl of London," he said. "She is a young girl in an old man's house."

"He is your friend!"

"He's an old goat – as I think you know," he said. "Be wary of him, Cordelia. Also, he is a terrible poker player. I empty his pockets on a regular basis."

It was a pleasant walk and once again, Cordelia courted scandal by going alone. Both Geoffrey and Ruby grimaced and exchanged glances. Cordelia knew that Geoffrey expected to be hauling her dead and robbed body out of a ditch at the rate she was carrying on. She ignored their protestations and sallied forth just after lunch.

She took her parasol, light long gloves, and a bag that rested in the crook of her arm. In the bag was a lurid novel and also her notebook.

For Freda Carter-Hall was to be the first of her interviewees, and her new project was beginning right now.

* * *

The Carter-Halls lived in a fine old house, with a sweeping driveway through a tall pair of gates which stood open. She walked up the steps to the portico, admiring the two bay trees in terracotta pots that stood either side of the door. One tree half-masked a locked letterbox attached to the wall. She rang the bell and stepped back, smiling and ready to be convivial and social.

And waited.

She expected a steward or butler, but it was a woman with a pointed nose who opened the door at last. She was dressed in dark, sombre clothing, and had a bunch of keys by her belt. She looked Cordelia up and down, and did not speak.

"Good afternoon," Cordelia said. "I wonder if Mrs Carter-Hall is at home?"

The housekeeper blinked in surprise. "Oh. I don't rightly know. I shall enquire. Wait."

And she disappeared, leaving Cordelia in shock on the doorstep with the door shut in her face.

She wavered. She had some calling cards in her bag, which she might leave on the hall table – if she were given the chance! She began to pull one free when the door was opened once more.

"She says she is here," the housekeeper said. "So, please, come in. Who might I say is calling?"

"Cordelia, Lady Cornbrook."

Using her title had the same effect as a slap in the face from a dead trout might have done. The housekeeper appeared to grow seven inches and her face went rigid. "Immediately, my lady. Sorry, my lady. Yes."

Yet it was still fully five minutes before Cordelia was shown into a day room. It was opulently furnished, evidently to demonstrate the Carter-Halls' riches to visitors.

Unlike the restrained elegance of Hugo's regency-inspired room, this was a place that screamed "Look! Money!" There were large portraits of the family on the walls, framed in heavy moulded gilt, all clamouring for attention in a higgledy-piggledy scramble, and a rash of spindly-legged tables that bristled with vases and ornaments. The overall colour scheme was "burgundy with a dash of gold" offset by "dark mahogany and rich green", and it was a place that would induce headaches in the frail and elderly within moments.

Somewhere among the frippery and lack of taste was a female figure, dressed much like the fireplace in unnecessary layers of bows and decoration. She was at an angle across a sofa, so that she was almost lying on it, and she half-rose but sank back almost straight away, exhausted. Her repose showed she was clearly unlaced. "My good lady Cordelia," she whispered throatily. "How awfully nice of you to come to see poor little me."

"Freda," she said, trying to match up this current vision with the flighty and lively woman she'd met at Hugo's soiree. "Are you quite well?" If she was unwell, the housekeeper should have declared her to be "not at home."

144

But then, Cordelia thought, *the housekeeper ought to have known her mistress's intentions right from the start, without having to check. Was it even the housekeeper? Or some random vagabond wandered in from the highway?*

"Oh, yes, Cordelia, quite well," Freda whispered. "Do, come over, sit down here near to me. Mrs Vale will be back with some refreshments soon. I hope."

Cordelia found a wide pink chair and dragged it to Freda. She still wore her bonnet and gloves and should have kept them on for a visit like this, but the room was stiflingly hot. Somewhat awkwardly, she stripped them off and laid them on a nearby table. She could overlook the improprieties. It didn't seem as if Freda would note it, or mind at all. If she could lie there without a corset, Cordelia could turn cartwheels through the room, really.

Freda was pale, but her eyes were sparkling and rimmed with red. She had a familiar languidity about her that spoke of laudanum or some cordial or elixir that contained the popular medicine. Nevertheless, Cordelia decided to press on with her plan.

She said, "Freda, I've come to you because I think you might be able to help me. I have a new direction! I am to become a woman of letters. I am embarked on a project to collect the regional recipes of each part of Britain. I have noticed, as I have travelled, that different areas–"

"Oh, travel!" Freda said, her head rolling from side to side. "How wonderful it would be to travel! Don't you think?"

"Yes, absolutely. And I am fascinated by the variation we see. When I was in town yesterday, I saw a man frying eels and they jumped and skipped in the pan as if they were alive still, and I thought–"

"Oh, goodness, eels!" Freda curled her lip and narrowed her eyes, letting her pale hand flutter to her throat in affection. "How dreadful."

Cordelia saw that she was not going to get anywhere. She glanced towards the door but there was no sign of the housekeeper with any refreshments. "Freda, my dear, might you ring for Mrs Vale…"

"Oh! Oh! She is such a slattern, that one. Of course! Of course!" But that necessitated rising, and she only managed to sit on the edge of the sofa before falling back once more. Cordelia herself went to the bells and rang, choosing both the kitchen and the housekeeper's room.

Cordelia stayed standing, and looked around the overdone room. In other circumstances she would have suggested they walk in the gardens but Freda could barely sit up. The house was deathly quiet. She said, "I believe you have children?"

Freda swept her hand from her throat, and waved it vaguely in the air before letting it drop. "Oh, yes, a few," she said as if unsure of the exact amount.

In Cordelia's experience, most women loved to talk of their offspring. It was something she had been trained to ask about, with the corresponding instruction to not talk at wearisome length about her own, if she were ever to have them. But Freda's extreme reticence was unusual. "How wonderful to be so blessed," she said, watching Freda's reaction.

Freda showed no response at all. "Yes," she said dully. "Ah! Here you are, Mrs Vale, at last. Thank you."

Mrs Vale brought in a tray of tea, and some small cakes arranged on a plate. She also glanced at Freda, who nodded. She disappeared, and Cordelia offered to pour the tea, but just as she did so, Mrs Vale came back with a small bottle and two glasses.

"Tea is a wonderful drink," Freda said, "but on hot days like these, one needs a little extra to struggle through the oppression, don't you find?"

The worst of the oppression would be cured by simply opening a window, not a bottle, but Cordelia merely nodded. She continued to pour the tea but Freda drank only the bright spirit that she poured into her glass. She poured some for Cordelia as well, but Cordelia made a show of politely sipping the burning liquor before setting it to one side.

"How many children do you have?" Cordelia asked, curious about Freda's lack of maternal instinct.

"Four at the moment," she said. "But one might die at any time." She said it flatly.

"Oh. Oh, how dreadful. I am sorry to hear that." Now Cordelia could forgive her dulled senses; who would not seek solace in opium? It was a dreadful statement.

Freda shrugged slightly, as if she was talking about the price of cotton. "She is young. Not yet five years old. And anyway, all my babies die young. It becomes a habit. Oh, except the ones that have lived, obviously."

It was almost as if she expected it. Cordelia's belly

clenched. "And what does the doctor say?"

"There is little point sending for a man who demands money yet cannot promise results," she said. "What a funny business is medicine, don't you think?"

"It is not a business…"

"We pay them, though, do we not? So – business, nothing more. How strange it is. Come, you will have another glass?"

Cordelia shook her head, but Freda poured herself a fresh drink and knocked it back as if it had been spring water. The alcohol was lending her a fire, and she was growing more animated. She sat up straight, her face flushing more red as she began to point at the objects in the room, randomly narrating their particular histories.

"Now, you see, this tea set, isn't it fine? I have a cousin who is in India, you know, and he sends back the most amazing things. And there, that sculpture, the bronze bull; Ewatt was in Spain and brought it home."

"Do you not travel with him?"

Freda pouted and now her husky voice was rising and taking on a whining tone. "No, he never takes me anywhere. Why, not even to London! I do so miss London. Oh, the balls, the parties. The shops! I love to shop. Instead I am forced to live here, where nothing ever happens and no one ever comes. No one interesting, anyway."

Cordelia tipped her chin up and stared steadily at Freda.

Freda was oblivious to her insult. "I am positive I shall simply fade away here, unknown and unremarked, while he dances in the cities of Europe. It is just *not fair.*"

Frankly, Cordelia thought, *I should not wish to take a drunken, opium-addled complainer such as yourself anywhere either. I can almost forgive Ewatt his indiscretions.* "There are some people of note here," she said mildly. "Do you not see the doctor's wife?"

"Oh, what, that goody-two-shoes? Miss Perfect and her perfect husband. Ah, Cordelia, when I see either of them, I feel so … so … small. Judged. Judged, and found wanting, as if they have the answers to anything! What good is outdoor activity and open air and vegetables? We will all die, Lady Cornbrook. We shall all die, no matter how many peaches one eats."

"How true." Cordelia nodded sympathetically and rose to her feet. She reached for her bonnet and gloves and plastered a polite smile on her face as she dressed for the outside once more. "Thank you so much for your hospitality."

Freda's attention seemed to sharpen. She pursed her coral-pink mouth. "Oh! Do not say you are leaving so soon!" She reached out, almost clawing like a reptile towards Cordelia.

"I must begin my research. My project, you know, as I said..."

"Oh! Yes, yes! Why, sit down, tell me more about it. It sounded marvellous. Um. Eels, was it not?"

"Not quite," Cordelia said. "Perhaps I will tell you another time."

Freda managed to get to her feet at last, and stood there, swaying. She looked ready to cry. "You have only just arrived." The loneliness was cascading off her, now. "I have completed an embroidery. Come, come and see it. It's in the garden room. You simply must. You will love it!"

"I should be delighted. Perhaps I might return at another date..." Cordelia inched her way backwards towards the door that led to the hallway. "However, I regret to say that I have some other engagements to attend to."

"It will take but a moment!" Freda pressed the bells

by the fireplace, mashing a few at random, determined to stall Cordelia. Cordelia had backed into the door and felt the handle at her back.

She smiled as kindly as she could. She had the handle in her hand behind her, and Freda before her, looking quite wild. She took one step forward to open the door as she moved. Freda looked ready to pounce upon her and drag her towards the fireplace, and suddenly Cordelia felt a prickling sense of danger, of something not quite right. She nodded and gabbled one more pleasantry, and turned, launching herself without looking into the hallway.

Whereupon she collided with Ewatt Carter-Hall, who was bending to take off his riding boots, and sent him sprawling to the tiles in a messy heap of tweed and curses.

CHAPTER FOURTEEN

As soon as Ewatt sat up and saw who had cannoned into him, he reined back his profanities, and instead he began to laugh. His legs were splayed out straight in front of him and he rested back on his hands, looking like a child playing on the beach.

"Lady Cornbrook, you make a magnificent entrance!" he boomed.

"I am *so* sorry," she said. She stepped forward and held out her hand.

His eyebrows shot up in surprise at her offer, but he accepted, and she helped to haul him to his feet. "Goodness. There is some uncommon power in you," he said, slowly.

She knew she ought to be embarrassed about it, and apologise for her woeful lack of femininity. But she could not be bothered with all that.

"Thank you," she said, as if it were a fine compliment. "Are you injured?"

"Oh no," he said, brushing his trouser legs down with exaggerated care. "The floor broke my fall."

She laughed, and he smiled, and their moment was immediately shattered by Freda appearing hard at Cordelia's elbow. She grabbed Cordelia's upper arm and leaned in for support. The sour smell of alcohol and something else, some tinge of sweat, was heavy upon her.

"Ewwwatt," she whined out, like a petulant schoolgirl. "*Do* tell Lady Cornbrook that she is to stop for dinner!"

Cordelia widened her eyes and shot Ewatt a startled look. Dinner would be a few hours away. She could not cope with much more of Freda's company. "Oh, I am honoured, but as I said, I have matters which need my attention and I am late already—"

Freda stamped her foot, which was rather ineffectual as a dramatic gesture, her soft slipper making but a dull thud. Cordelia pulled away from her grasp, leaving Freda to rest her weight on the doorframe instead.

Ewatt was not looking pleased at his wife's state. "You

look *tired*, dear," he said, and Cordelia recognised a couple's code in his words. "I shall ring for Kitty and have you taken to bed to rest."

"I shall not go!"

Cordelia began to move towards the main door and Ewatt accompanied her. In lieu of any butler or steward present, he took on the duties to show her out himself. Freda remained by the receiving room, and had begun to cry, her sobs increasing in volume as no one took any notice of her.

He opened the door and as he ushered her through it, he bent his head towards hers. "I can only apologise for my wife's current indisposition. I thank you for your company but I wonder if, perhaps, she would be better served with a period of rest and calming solitude…"

"I am sorry that I have inconvenienced her," she replied smoothly. "It is a trying situation but temporary, I am sure. Things must be very difficult for her at the moment, and if I can render any assistance, please do let me know."

Ewatt paused, and looked confused. "Why would things be … never mind. Lady Cornbrook, how did you get here?"

"I walked. And I shall walk back. Thank you, and once again, my apologies."

"I see. Right. No, no, you shall not walk back alone. I will not hear of it. Let me organise my footwear; one moment."

She looked down and realised that he was in his stockinged feet. He had been removing his boots when she had fallen into him, and they had been thrown clean across the hallway. She was too busy laughing to voice her protests, and he slithered away across the tiles like a skater, retrieving his boots and returning to her swiftly.

"Ewatt, Ewatt!"

But he ignored his wife, and closed the door behind him.

Well, so she was not to shake him off. She walked down the steps and he fell alongside her, offering his arm. She hitched her bag around on her elbow and refused. "I find I keep my balance better unencumbered."

"Ah, so a man is a mere encumbrance. That reveals much about you, Lady Cornbrook."

"That you seek to read meanings into everyday things

reveals much about yourself," she shot back.

"Well played. Now, what did you mean, back there? You said that my poor, ailing wife was finding things difficult. That the situation was temporary. Has she unburdened herself to you? Sometimes she is prone to fancies. Not all that she says has meaning."

"Indeed. You may rest assured that no confidences have been broken, I am sure of it. No. I merely alluded to the sad illness of one of your children."

"Oh, that." And Ewatt spoke as dully as Freda had done, staring off into the distance, with a set and passive face.

"Your youngest, I believe?"

"Yes. She is frail, like her mother. Alas, there is nothing to be done. We all struggle on, do we not, with our secret hardships."

"And the doctor has no hope to offer?" she probed.

"Oh, we have seen this pattern of sickening and decline before, and it hardly seems worth troubling the good doctor when he has so much to do. He has so much very important work. He is quite the model of diligence, do you not find? Tell me, what is your opinion of our esteemed doctor?"

"He does, as you say, seem the very model of all a doctor should be," she replied cautiously. Was that an undercurrent of sarcasm in Ewatt's words? She was not entirely sure. "However, I have had little cause to converse with him."

"Well, no, you wouldn't have," he said. "Unless you believe in the bracing properties of cold air and the healing miasmas to be found under trees."

"You make him sound almost pagan."

"Oh, he calls it science, but science, as we all know, is a thing of sparks and glass flasks and liquids that change colour. But he goes into sickrooms and opens the windows." He said it as if it was the most absurd thing he had ever heard.

"How interesting," she said, thinking that it was rather sensible in many cases. "But that is the advice in most circles, you know. Ventilation is considered very sanitary. We must guard against the build-up of carbonic acid, so I have heard. Anyway, how does the town take to him?"

"Carbonic acid? Pfft. As for the town, well, he's a doctor, so he's a gentleman. They fear him and admire him and don't understand him. And anyway, most of them cannot afford him and if they could, they would rather choose to visit an old fenland mother and get a cure of snail oil or some such. And keep their windows closed."

"That would be the common people, yes," she said. "But what of the better class?"

"Here? My dear lady, there is very little better class. There is me, and your Hugo, and the handful of worthies that you have already met. Why, the better class has doubled with the arrival of the coroner and the sheriff!"

She overlooked the reference to "her" Hugo. To maintain conversation about Doctor Arnall, who was intriguing her more and more, she said, "Do you know, I heard the strangest thing today. I was in the Post Office and the clerk there said that the doctor had been sending letters."

"The clerk is a notorious gossip," Ewatt said. His pace quickened, and she remembered that Ewatt himself had been in there. No doubt he would know that if the clerk had spoken of another, then it was as likely that Ewatt would have been spoken of, too.

Not wishing to cause him any embarrassment, she did not speak further. They walked on and soon they could see the stone pillars of Hugo's estate.

Then Ewatt said, "And what was so interesting about the doctor's letters?"

"That they were all to Liverpool, but not to family or friends. Unless…" Now she was as bad as the clerk for spreading rumours. She stopped herself.

But she had said too much to hide anything from Ewatt now. "Go on."

"Well, he had written to a number of hospitals and prisons there! What do you make of that?"

"Oh." Ewatt's speed slackened. "So, to whom was he writing?"

"I know not. But he comes from Liverpool. Perhaps he was writing to old colleagues?"

"In hospitals, maybe. But prisons? Well, now. That is very interesting. And did any other information reveal itself to the clerk?"

She knew he was asking if the clerk had gossiped about Ewatt himself. Discretely, she said, "No, not at all. Though he was a garrulous old chap."

"Indeed he is. And I would offer you counsel, if I may." They had reached the bottom of the steps to the entrance of Hugo's house, and halted. Ewatt reached out to take her hands. "There are people in this town who seek only to further their own ends. As a visitor, you do not know of their histories and their individual grievances. I would, at all times, exercise the greatest caution in your dealings with them."

"How will I know which ones to be cautious about?"

"Oh," he said, with a sudden hearty guffaw. "Mistrust the whole seething lot of them! Tis the easiest way. No one here is what they seem."

"Excepting you," she said.

"Oh, as for myself, I lack the wit and energy to be anything other than what you now see. A dreadful old fool, but a sincere one. Now, inside with you, and next time you wish to come visiting, do send word ahead. My poor Freda … well, you understand, I am sure."

"I do," she responded, thinking, *no, I do not. But I want to find out. For I trust you about as much as I trust anyone else. Which it to say, very little.*

"Good day, Lady Cornbrook."

She nodded and the door to the house had opened before she was halfway up the stairs. Hugo Hawke kept a far tighter rein on his staff than Ewatt Carter-Hall. She glanced back as she slipped inside, but the banker had already departed from view.

CHAPTER FIFTEEN

Cordelia sat at the dressing table, her hands folded patiently in her lap. Ruby was behind her, attending to her hair, pulling most of the mousey-blonde curls back into a bun, before working loose some tendrils to cascade artfully around her face.

It was a style that went very well on a young woman, she thought. Now, as a widow in her thirties, she thought a different hairstyle would suit her more. For a while she had affected caps and other dressings, that the much older women favoured, but they had aged her dramatically and even people she didn't know would take her aside for some excruciatingly awkward "quiet advice."

So here she was, stuck in some middle land of not-young and not-old, when others her age were either at home with their growing families, or clinging to their youth with layers of powder while their children were raised by nurses and strangers.

And then, she thought, *there was Freda*. "I went to the Carter-Halls' house today," she said, startling Ruby who was used to performing this task in contemplative silence.

"Yes, my lady."

"She has been preying on my mind," Cordelia said. It was true. She needed to talk about it, and it hardly mattered to whom she spoke; even her maid. Their relationship was shifting by imperceptible degrees every time she spoke to Ruby like this. She no longer cared. "The mistress of the house is in a sorry way, and it has an effect on the whole household. There was no one to open the door to me. When someone did come, the housekeeper, she had had no orders from the mistress for the day as to whether she was at home or not. There was dust on the cornices and a smear of dirt on the tiles in the entrance hall. The curtains and drapes were but half-withdrawn, and that untidily so."

"Oh."

"Altogether, it was a house of no direction and under no command. I do feel for the master of the house; it ought to be his place of sanctuary and comfort, yet it is a house of … well, I hesitate to say *disorder,* but I can see why he travels so much."

"Hm."

Cordelia watched Ruby's deft fingers in the reflection of the looking-glass. They did not falter from their familiar task. Her face was downcast, and her curling mouth set in a line, an unusual expression for her.

"Ruby, you are biting your lip."

"I am concentrating, my lady."

Cordelia continued to watch her, and though Ruby did not make eye contact, she knew she was under scrutiny, and eventually she broke.

"My lady, if I may…"

"Please do. I would be fascinated to know your opinions." She knew it sounded sarcastic but she didn't mean it so. "I really would," she added, making it worse rather than better.

Ruby frowned. "Well, my lady. Well. There is a footman here, that I know, ahem, and his sister is a maid at the Carter-Halls'. She stays there only for the obligation she feels to the mistress there. Were it other, she would have fled long ago, with the rest of the staff who would not be party to the master's … habits."

Cordelia stiffened. "His *habits?* He is a man, with a man's usual failings, of course." *How we all excuse their weaknesses when we are supposed to be the weaker sex,* Cordelia thought.

"Oh," Ruby said, her hands waving in the air. "Oh, yes, the usual failings, no doubt. But there is no call for a man to call his wife mad, insane, and lock her up simply because she is tiresome to him. She is not mad. There is no call for a man to let his children wither and die because he will not pay for the doctor. He never has! Though he is happy enough to pay into a burial club – now what does *that* tell you?"

"I am shocked!" Cordelia said. "I am appalled at your accusations though, if true, I would also be shocked at what your accusations contain. Have you any proof?"

"I would need double the proof of a rich man to make any progress, and be heeded," she muttered.

Cordelia opened and closed her mouth, and sat in dumb silence for a moment.

Ruby finished Cordelia's hair and sprayed a light mist of scented rosewater around her bare neck and shoulders.

As if she had not just spoken dreadfully ill of another, she patted a curl into place and said, "There, now, my lady. You are dressed for dinner."

* * *

Hugo was distant and distracted at dinner. He was tired, and she thought that he might be suffering a protracted hangover. He made polite conversation, and listened half-attentively to her gabbled, excited plans for writing a series of cookbooks that explored regional flavours and methods. He said that it sounded interesting, and showed no interest at all. He reassured her that the fault was all his, told her to make full use of his kitchen and his cook, apologised for his lack of sparkle, and took his leave early.

She was slightly perturbed. After all, he had encouraged her to stay on for longer. They had yet to discuss the ending of his trusteeship and the loss of her home. Maybe, she thought, her plans to be self-sufficient had angered him. He hadn't proposed to her again for at least three days. She wavered between excitement at the idea of being some kind of travelling writer, and deep despondency that Clarfields was soon to be turned over to Hugo. Marriage to him would keep her house. It was the logical solution.

Oh, we women are supposed to be illogical, she told herself. *Why could she not have Clarfields without the added burden of Hugo? It was not fair.*

She was wearing her formal evening wear, and she felt restless, as if she were all dressed up for an event that had not happened. On other evenings, when they had dined alone but for the bevy of servants silently along the walls, they had laughed and joked; often they had played cards, or he would read scurrilous stories from the newspapers he had sent from London. Always, they skirted the big issue. What was he waiting for?

It was late and night was falling, but she was not ready to sleep yet. She stepped into the cold, unheated hallway. Someone had lit alternate lamps along the wall, but it felt empty and unloved without people in the space. *This was a house for parties,* she thought. It was very much suited to Hugo Hawke. She wondered what his next event was going to be; she hoped it was to be a card game evening, and resolved to begin dropping heavy hints.

She walked up the stairs, and along the long corridor, her skirts rustling against the dark wood display cases that stood against the wall. At the far end, someone appeared in black and white, saw her, and melted back into the shadows again; a servant, who knew they ought not to be seen.

Cordelia found her rooms as still and quiet as the rest of the house. Everything slumbered under a layer of inertia. Ruby obviously did not expect her back from dinner so soon. She collected a heavy cloak, one that she favoured for travelling, and swung it around her shoulders. She decided she would walk in the gardens. She had seen a bright moon, almost full, riding high in the sky and she thought that it would illuminate the blue and white flowers to good effect.

The scene in the peaceful gardens did not disappoint. Under the silver light, all was washed out and bleached, save for any blooms which were blue. They glowed, their moment of glory finally come as they could outshine the blowsy reds and pinks which dominated the daytime.

How is it that shadows and darkness bring new things to light, she thought, and repeated the sentence a few times so that she remembered it. She could write that down in her notebook and use it later. She was excited, again, about her new plan, now she looked at the flowers and plants. There was a fashion for instructional manuals about cookery and household management, designed to help young wives with aspirations but little knowledge. Cordelia thought that her books would be a combination of practical information and interesting study. *I could write a whole series*, she thought. She could travel the country, her research the perfect excuse to go visiting. That would be a far more exciting way to spend her life than chasing a husband just to seem respectable! Yes, she would refuse Hugo, once and for all. Let him have Clarfields. She would make her own way.

She felt sick with sorrow.

She came to a large, soft-leaved plant; sage, with its tall spikes of flowers. The scent filled the air and she thought about the uses of it in the kitchen, especially in stuffing meats.

And in the sickroom, also, she thought. That brought to mind Doctor Donald Arnall and his enigmatic ways. But how much of his deeds and words were truly strange and how much was simply the filtered perception of other people? She wanted to speak to the man himself. The way to do that, she realised, was to befriend his wife. She hoped that Mrs Arnall would be more congenial and easier to talk to than Mrs Carter-Hall.

There was the snap of a twig somewhere far to her left. She paused. A servant, on a tryst? A poacher, taking a short-cut? The still-uncaught murderer, perhaps, intent on more evil. Or maybe just Geoffrey, lurking in the shadows to keep his watchful eye on her, bound to her by more than staff loyalty; bound to her by history and secrets, as was Mrs Unsworth, in her particular way.

She shook it off, but did turn and began to make her way to the safety of the house. She approached from the back, passing around the outbuildings by the back door of the kitchen area. The soft, pale light from a window was broken momentarily by a dark figure passing in front of it, stealthily bent over carrying a bundle in its arms. It wore a flat cap and from the shape of its face, must have been muffled in scarves or cloth. It walked on the grass rather than the gravel and disappeared between two store buildings. She stopped. She did not want to follow, and be cornered by it in a passageway.

But she also wanted to know who it was. She took a step forward, her heart pounding and her mind telling her she was utterly, utterly, foolish.

"My lady!"

She jumped, bit back her squeal into a cough, and turned to face Geoffrey. "My lady," he said again. "I apologise for startling you."

"Oh. Yes. Well," she stammered, discomforted.

"Allow me to walk you to the main entrance," he said, very firmly. "It is dark and it is not right for you to be alone in this. Anybody might be abroad."

"Anybody likely is," she said.

"I'm sorry?"

"Nothing." She accepted his offer of his arm and let him take her around the house. Such things would not do in the light of day. But it was dark, and she was foolish, and he was probably correct.

CHAPTER SIXTEEN

Everything changed.

All her plans and resolutions were turned on their heads, and she had no warning of it.

The following day, she threw herself into her project. Hugo cleared a table for her in the library, a well-apportioned room next to his study. She laid out great sheets of paper upon which she had drawn sprawling plans and lists of ideas. That morning Hugo stood at her shoulder and asked her well-meaning questions which showed a total lack of understanding but, at least, a pleasing willingness to be involved.

At lunch, they talked idly of other matters. Ewatt Carter-Hall had absented himself again recently, according to Hugo, taking the train from the new railway station in Cambridge to spend a day or two attending to business in

London. Mrs Hurrell was still locked up while the coroner and the sheriff ate their way through the inn's specialities and argued about how a woman could be a murderer. Oh, a woman could be a poisoner all right - but to fell a man with a blow, now that was something else. It thrilled the local gossips.

It was a grey and thunderous afternoon, and unexpectedly, Hugo sought her out in the library. It was late and approaching five. His reticent demeanour had vanished. Now, he leaned casually against a cabinet and folded his arms, one leg cocked and bent, and his whole body in a sinuous curve of suppressed energy.

"How goes the book?" he asked.

She saw at once that he had been drinking.

"Very well," she said. "Mrs Unsworth and your cook have been most accommodating." Actually, Mrs Unsworth had said nothing but had glowered and frowned, and Hugo's cook had been confused but keen. "I have found a fascinating old book of recipes, here in your library, written by a previous mistress of this house, and she details some of the unique foods of this area. There are four different ways of making chestnut stuffing! You must send me some chestnuts this winter so that I might try the recipe myself."

"Why not return to collect them yourself?" he said, his eyebrows waggling. "If you want my nuts, you must…"

"Hugo, stop that. You are being rude and you know it."

He spread his hands wide in artificial innocence. "I apologise for my unwitting transgression. What else have you found?"

"There is a cheese that is sold in Stilton and parts around there, which they call the English parmesan," she said. "It sounds fascinating and I would dearly love to procure some. I have sent my boy, Stanley, to ask around."

"I believe I have had it; it's a smelly one, I must warn you. It is quite matured."

"Some things are better mature," she said.

"But not to the point of becoming thick with mould," he pointed out. "Still, I shall put word about for you."

There was a silence that stretched out. Cordelia began to pile up her books and papers, tidying away ready for another day.

Hugo continued to slouch against the cabinet. He watched her hungrily.

Then they both spoke at once.

"Hugo, I–"

"Cordelia. Listen."

She stopped, and listened.

"Let's not beat about the bush. You know I can't do fancy language. I suppose I ought to spend a few hours waxing lyrical about your eyes or something. I'm not going to do that."

His attitude was casual, she noted, but now his hands were balled into tight, white fists as he struggled for words.

He continued. "Clarfields is mine. It's a big old empty house, and I am going to sell it."

It's not empty! I live there! She could not help herself. She glared at him.

"But I would be letting my old friend down if you were cast out. The best thing to do is for you to marry me. We've been playing at proposals since you came here, Cordelia, but we both know it's a matter of logic. Flirting is fun. Even I can do that. But it's not real. Let's be adult. A quick wedding, and there we are."

This was it. It was time to tell him of her change of plan. She waved her hand at her neatly-stacked books. "I appreciate everything you've done for me, Hugo. But see, this new project of mine … I am going to travel, and write books."

Now it was his turn to glare. He barked out a short, dismissive laugh. "Oh, Cordelia, you stupid, silly, vainglorious woman. It is another passing fad of yours, a fancy, nothing more. You'll wake up tomorrow and decide instead to sail to the Africas and chart the stars, or some other nonsense. Nothing you have done has ever achieved anything. Why, you don't even have children! That's the most basic thing, the most important thing, that a woman must do. And I am giving you that chance. Home. Family."

The Angel in the House.

Cordelia was not built to be an angel.

"Here?" she said, trying to keep the quiver out of her voice. "Marry you. Live here. Sell Clarfields. Give up my dreams."

"Dreams? Cordelia, can't you see that they are just a substitute for what you really should be doing with your life?"

She folded her arms, twitched her hands, unfolded them again, half-turned away, sucked in her breath, and tried very hard to not throw anything. She could have hurled a table at the man. As she fought for control, he came up to her, but stopped short of touching her. He waited, a few feet away, and there was such an expression of patronising sympathy on his face that she choked as she spoke.

"Hugo. Thank you for your *offer*. I regretfully decline. I have independent means. I have an aim. I have friends. You may have Clarfields but you shall not have me. And I apologise – I truly do – if I have led you on, in any way. For in truth I did not know what I wanted until recently."

And then he grabbed her, seizing her upper arms. "Just like that? You will leave?"

"I can go this very night if you wish."

His face was very close to her. She considered fighting him off, but was it worth it? She didn't think he would truly harm her. He pressed her backwards, so that her bustle jammed against the table, and leaned his body along hers. "I did not mean, leave here. You will leave Clarfields?"

"Yes, I will leave Clarfields." Saying it out loud caused her pain. She did not want to leave. In spite of it all, in spite of her defiant words, that was the one true place of sanctuary that she had. She had not realised how much she loved it until the reality of losing it was upon her.

And he saw her weakness. "Marry me ... and you can keep Clarfields."

In an instant, she saw *his* weakness. "Why did you wish to sell it, Hugo?"

"It is a burden, a drain on my finances."

"It is my finances that you want, is it not? At the moment of engagement, all my wealth becomes yours."

"I admire you, Cordelia," he said, taking on a wheedling tone. Suddenly, he let go of her. "Come. This ... discussion ... is thirsty work. Let us sit, and take a drink, and explore this further."

"There is nothing to explore," she said stubbornly, but she followed his pointing arm to the wing-back chairs that stood either side of the empty fireplace. He went to a decanter and poured a sherry for her, and a strong brandy for himself.

They sat for a moment. She thought about his proposition. *Marry him, and keep Clarfields.*

He watched her. "You are considering it, are you not?"

She would be foolish not to mull it over.

She said, "You're a gambling man, are you not?"

"Do you mean to say, that you think I wish to marry you only to pay off my debts?"

Indeed so. She inclined her head.

"I do not," he said. "Unlike foolish Ewatt, I set my limits. I may wager high but I can walk away. I often do. You have seen that yourself, Cordelia."

It was true, and she allowed herself a smile. They had bet for small things, trifles, in their evening card games. She had usually beaten him, and he had never been goaded into more and more games to recoup his losses. She admired that about him.

"I have," she conceded. "I mean only to say, perhaps this is something that cannot be solved by talking..."

He narrowed his eyes and took a deep slurp of his drink. "No."

"Hugo, perhaps—"

"I know what you propose, Cordelia. No. I shall not put Clarfields on the outcome of a game of cards! Marry me if you wish to stay there. Reject me to wander, rootless, a discarded widow, as your beauty fades. You are running out of time, Cordelia, and soon you will be without prospects. No man can gain a title by marrying you, and it will die with you. Estate-less. Landless. Your stocks and shares, yes, they will give you a living. But society will not have you. No one shall have you. Marriage will give you everything that you want. Not a game of cards."

It would not be that simple. He would have demands of her. Expectations. And even then, he might still sell Clarfields. He *did* want her wealth. She would have no say in the matter.

She stood up in a rush, and said, "No. I will leave, tonight."

He stood up to match her. "You will not."

"You cannot–"

"We have guests. Ewatt will be here. He is returned from town; he went only to Cambridge, not London. I had word earlier. And also the coroner, John Barron, is joining us for dinner."

It was news to her, but then, why would she be consulted in matters of his household. "Then you shall entertain them alone."

He raised one eyebrow. "Barron has information about the case, no doubt."

"So?"

"And it is to be roast pork."

"So?"

"And perhaps cards afterwards…"

"I will leave in the morning," she snapped, and stormed from the room.

* * *

"It will be a *mixed* card game, will it not?" Ruby demanded, later, when Cordelia went to the kitchens to talk to Mrs Unsworth about the cancellation of the grand cheese quest.

"I shall be there, so yes, of course. It will be entirely respectable."

Mrs Unsworth sat heavily on a stool, her face grey but her nose strangely pink. She narrowed her eyes but did not speak.

"Well, quite," Cordelia said into the silence. "And we are to leave. We must get back to Clarfields and … and … make preparations." She could not go on. She would deal with that when she returned. Falsely bright, she turned to Mrs Unsworth. "So, there is no sign of the cheese?"

182

"None at all," Mrs Unsworth said shortly.

"Right. Ruby, I shall need you upstairs. We have much to do."

"My lady."

* * *

But the evening was not respectable at all. At dinner, there were too many bottles of wine on the table and too few that were left full by the time they left the room. John Barron was a corpulent man who refused to discuss the murder at all, at least while they ate. Ewatt was the most garrulous, and he kept them entertained for minutes at a time with his stories and jokes.

Afterwards, Cordelia withdrew to let the men smoke for a short time. Now she was alone in the drawing room, and wandered between the chairs and tables, feeling a pent-up rage build within. *Tomorrow, Clarfields. Next week, next month ... what? Where?*

Hugo called for her, loudly, his voice thick with intoxication. She came back through, and he took her arm firmly. They wandered a circuitous course, followed by John

Barron and Ewatt, towards a large room beyond the library and behind his study. In his bachelor rut, he had rooms that defied categorisation and convention; this was ostensibly his "games room" but there were a few comfortable sofas, card tables, a drinks cabinet, a shelf of books, a globe of the known world and a small clockwork model of a screw-propeller ocean-going liner. It was a comfortable but very male space. It smelled of wood and cigars with the faint tinge of unwashed socks.

She felt that she ought not be there.

The room was on the ground floor, and they had to cross the mouth of the passageway that ran to the kitchens at the back. Cordelia turned her head as they went across the cold, draughty opening, the green baize door standing brazenly open. At the far end of the corridor, defiantly in her domain, stood Mrs Unsworth. She gave Cordelia a long, hard stare, and Cordelia felt her wine-reddened cheeks deepen with a blush of shame.

It ought to be Mrs Unsworth who hung her head in deference and sadness, Cordelia thought, and snatched her gaze away. She was in no mood to be challenged by a servant with delusions of grandeur.

Hugo had not noticed a thing. He bounced off the wall and ricocheted back which took him neatly into the games room, where he flung himself onto a sofa.

Ewatt grabbed a bottle of brandy, and began to pour. Barron's fat face was shiny and he eased himself into an over-stuffed chair.

Three men, and her.

She had to choose. Leave and meet propriety's standards – or stay, and get very drunk.

"Have you any wine?" she asked.

* * *

Ewatt had just returned from town, and he produced an expensive bottle of vintage wine from the carpet bag at his feet that the butler delivered to him when he called for it. Cordelia wondered if he had literally just stepped down from the carriage and had not even visited his house.

The men began to talk as if she were not there. Barron ploughed through the brandy quickly. Ewatt and Hugo indulged in a loud competition about the most expensive bottle of wine they had ever opened, and Ewatt bragged about the quails' eggs he had eaten that morning. Cordelia blatantly yawned and rolled her eyes. In between games of loo, they drank and they talked. Sometimes they paired off to play whist. Cordelia relaxed. It was her final night. The die was cast. She got drunk, and nothing mattered so much anymore.

All in all, it became a dreadful, disorderly and unbecoming evening of great fun.

But it began to fade, as all things do. Tiredness crept upon them all. The talk turned to darker things, and the matter of the murder in particular.

"They must charge Mrs Hurrell, and hang her, and there is an end of it!" Hugo said impatiently. "I do not see why they are dragging their feet over it. Barron, you know the process. What is going on?"

"I am the coroner, not the magistrate," he said. "I can tell you the death was suspicious. That is all. No one is bringing a prosecution, as far as I know."

"There was murder! They must not have enough evidence," Cordelia said. "And I for one would count it a grave injustice, for Mrs Hurrell is innocent."

"Poppycock! She was there at the scene," Ewatt said.

"But the murderer escaped out through the back," she said. "And they climbed the wall, and was away. Would not Mrs Hurrell have fled, too, if she had done the deed?"

"I can imagine someone getting into a fight with the lad in a beerhouse or inn," Hugo said, pointing his finger randomly around. "But why would someone seek this boy out and kill him? That is premeditated, is it not? That takes planning. Now, Mrs Hurrell was there, so I can imagine a fight. But for someone else to come into the house, and kill him? No. The lad was not so interesting that anyone could be bothered to go to the effort, surely."

Hugo sat back, then sat forward, belched and got unsteadily to his feet. "Excuse me, please. One moment. I must call to nature. No, a call of nature. That too."

"There are ladies present!" Ewatt admonished him.

"Plural? Cordelia and … well, you must speak of yourself," he said, and punched his friend on the shoulder as he passed on the way to leave the room.

Grown men, when drunk, regressed to young lads once more, she thought, then giggled, feeling rather schoolgirlish herself as the wine burbled through her body.

Barron rolled his eyes and picked up the now-empty

brandy bottle. "Damn him," he said. "He ought to have called for more." He got to his feet and stumbled out into the corridor.

"I have to thank you," Ewatt said as soon as they were alone. His face was glazed with the sweat of an evening of too much drink and food and laughter, but his eyes were fairly focused. "For your information about our good doctor Arnall."

"My information? Whatever do you mean?"

"That he was writing to Liverpool. You raised my suspicions. I had … I obtained … I took a chance to … well, Cordelia, Cordelia, I have discovered the most alarming thing about our doctor. He was married before!"

She overlooked his personal use of her first name. "Many people are married more than once."

"But what happened to his first wife?"

"I do not know."

"Exactly! Back in Liverpool, he was tied to an unhappy woman. Oh, he killed her, and I have seen the evidence, I have! And here he is, but the blood lust is upon him still, and he has killed again."

"Oh, come now. Why would *he* kill the lad?"

"They had argued. That is common knowledge. And once a man has killed, once a man has felt the thrill of his primal power, then of course, he will seek to do it again and again!"

"Is that so?"

"It is!" Ewatt assured her. "Much like hunting, I suppose. And wine. Once one has the taste for any power, it is in them. Deep inside them!" He slapped his own chest, and somehow managed to unbalance himself. He was clinging to the edge of the sofa when Hugo re-entered.

"Am I missing some circus tricks?" he said, and with a push of his hand he toppled Ewatt over entirely.

Barron was soon behind Hugo, and looked down on the prone figure of Ewatt with some distaste. Barron, for all his consumption, was not as drunk as the unfortunate banker.

Cordelia thought, *why has Ewatt not revealed these suspicions about the doctor? Why tell only me? He is drunk, of course. And not in seriousness.*

But she could not let the matter lie, whether Ewatt had jested or not. "Ewatt," she said, and that jolted him alert. He smiled as he regained his feet. "Tell me again about your thoughts on the doctor."

He waved his hand in the air. "Enough about this tedious murder! Who cares about that boy?"

"Exactly," she said. "No one does, but we must."

"I shall tell you what I care about. More wine. More brandy. More cards." He took one step to the table and stumbled.

Hugo grabbed him and hauled him upright. "Ewatt, you sozzled old sot, you can't even see, never mind play. I'll call for you to be taken home."

"No, no, Huuuugo…" Ewatt lapsed into song as Hugo dragged him to the door and called for assistance.

There was an awkward few moments as Cordelia and John Barron were left alone. She took her seat and played with her half-empty glass. It was time, she knew, to retire. The coroner made it very clear he was not going to converse with her. The door was left open, and soon Hugo returned. She rose as he re-entered the room.

"Thank you for a lovely evening," she said.

"You are not going!"

"Of course. I must. I need sleep, and tomorrow I…"

"Tomorrow you leave for good. You are quite set upon

this, then? You shall break my heart and your own … for spite?"

"I do not act out of spite! And I am not breaking your heart any more than you are breaking mine."

"But I do break yours," he said, more quietly, "for I take your house from you."

"You beast."

John Barron coughed politely but Cordelia ignored him. She clenched her fists and stared at Hugo, feeling hot and uncomfortably sweaty.

Hugo walked to the card table and picked up a deck, riffling through them casually. His steady was a surprise to her. He, too, had not drunk as much as Ewatt. He was still in control.

She did not feel in control at all.

"I want Clarfields," she said, quietly. He was going to take it from her.

"Marry me, then," he said.

"Never. Play me at cards. Let me have the chance of winning my home back."

Barron interrupted. "I have no idea what this is all about, but the good lady is challenging you to a card game,

Hawke. Why not, eh?"

Hugo fanned the cards out and then scooped them up with a flourish. "She will beat me," he said. "The match would not be fair."

"She is good at whist. Try poker."

"No." Hugo cocked his head and regarded her, a cunning smile coming onto his face. "You really do care about this murdered boy, don't you?"

"It's the principle of the thing," she said.

Both Barron and Hugo snorted. Hugo said, "So, here's a wager more to my liking."

A cold hand seemed to settle on the back of her neck. "Go on."

"Solve the murder yourself. Bring the killer to justice. Prove it was – or wasn't – Mrs Hurrell. If it wasn't, find out who it was."

"And then?"

"You keep Clarfields."

Barron was shaking his head but he clicked his fingers at Hugo. "Fetch me some paper, man. Let's do this thing properly."

Cordelia stood in a daze as a contract was drawn up

by the coroner. Within minutes, there it stood: the agreement that Clarfields would pass to her, in its entirety, should she solve the case.

"How long do I have?" she asked.

"I go north for the hunting in two weeks' time," Hugo said.

Barron looked up at her, his pen poised to witness their signatures. "Better get on with it, Lady Cornbrook," he said, and smiled.

CHAPTER SEVENTEEN

Ruby was singing.

Cordelia pulled the rich cotton sheets up and burrowed low in the wide, soft bed. The heavy curtains were pulled closed across the window, and the room was dark, but still the burgeoning day intruded into her thick and muzzy head.

She kept herself muffled up in the sheets and covers when she heard the bedroom door open. *Take the hint, take the hint,* she thought. *Go away.*

She couldn't hear footsteps on the luxurious carpets but she knew Ruby had come to the bedside by the clink of a tray being set down on the table. "Mr Peeble's Salts," Ruby said. "And some water, and some fruit, and a little bread. My lady. I understand we are not to be leaving after all. I have things in hand."

She heard the rustle of skirts and the door clicked

closed.

And then, distant singing once more.

The naughty maid. Cordelia struggled into a sitting position and looked at the tray, and allowed herself a smile. Ruby had potential, after all.

* * *

She spent the morning with her notebook and deep in introspection. The cookery book project? A mere trifle, just as they had all said.

No, the real business was now on. The murder!

By midday, Cordelia was back to her usual perky self, though there had been no sign of Hugo. She enquired after his health with his house steward, who remained perfectly impassive and professional and merely replied, "I shall pass on your good wishes." She hadn't actually wished him anything, good or bad, but it was clear that the man was not going to reveal the state of his master.

She went out to the stables and spotted Geoffrey talking to Stanley who was in the centre of a manège, lunging one of the horses.

She thought she would overhear him telling Stanley about horsemanship, or the duties of an aspiring coachman, but instead she heard Geoffrey halfway through a tirade about education and the common man. She went slowly and silently, the better to listen before she was spotted. Geoffrey had his back to her and was leaning on the wooden railings around the manège.

"I'll agree that there's a deal of money in it," Geoffrey was saying. "And I'll agree that some folks like us can't never get to the same places as folks like them. I ain't saying that the poor are the same as the rich. We are in body, yes, but not in other things. Because, happen that you or I suddenly came into all the wealth as they have – what then? We still would not be as them, would we? So there is more to it than money."

"A-a-ancestors," Stanley said, twirling in a slow circle, his eyes fixed on the trotting horse that was going in a circle around him.

"Ain't nobody have any more ancestors than anybody else, boy. It ain't all money and it ain't all to do with family, neither. It's them things, yes, but it's education. And it ain't just book-learning that I mean. It's the knowing of who is who and what to eat and what to wear and when to laugh and when to not laugh."

"I b-believe we are all equal under God," Stanley said. "But we have our allotted p-places. It is respect." He was breathing hard as he spun, and he clicked to bring the horse back down to a walk again. Cordelia could see that the horse was slightly favouring one of its hind legs.

"Mayhap we are," Geoffrey said. "As for that, under God, I don't know. But I tell you this, though. You like reading, but you want to be reading more than just your religious this and religious that. Or else you shall always be a servant and nothing more. Is that your place, your destiny, for ever?"

Now Stanley had slowed down he could look about him, and when he caught sight of Cordelia he nearly lost his pace with the horse. He reddened and coughed, and his stare alerted Geoffrey who glanced over his shoulder.

She went to his side and rested her arms on the wooden fence. "The mare is lame."

"Aye, she was. But Stanley here has done well with her care. We were resting her, and today we wanted to see how she fared. She is improving. Stanley, take her inside."

198

"S-sir."

"You're teaching him well," she said.

Geoffrey exhaled sharply and pushed himself away from the fence, standing upright and tall. "Aye, but do he listen?"

"I'm sure it all goes in."

"How long do we stay here? Yesterday we were to leave today. Today ... we are staying, I was told."

"We are staying. But for no more than a fortnight."

"And you are embarked on this plan to write recipe books?"

She could not hide her smile. "Perhaps." It would be a good cover story, she thought. "Or perhaps there are more stories than just those about food, here. I have heard some information about the doctor that I wish to investigate."

"Why?"

He really was the rudest man alive. She stopped herself from rolling her eyes at him. "If I could expose the true murderer, I could write that for the papers, and then as a book, and that would be something, would it not? I may write a book of regional recipes but it will be read and then

forgotten. This, though, would last. My name would go on."
Even as she said it, extemporising though she was, it seemed
like a convincing plan. She wasn't going to tell him it was
all on a wager to keep her house.

"Immortality ain't the best motivation, to my mind,"
Geoffrey said drily. "However, you are the mistress and I
am but a lowly and uneducated servant."

She narrowed her eyes at him and he had the defiance
to stare her back down. *Damn him.* "Keep the horses
exercised," she said curtly, and spun away to seek out Ruby.
She wanted her companionship on a walk to the Post Office.

* * *

"I need evidence," Cordelia said as they walked along
the now-familiar track to town.

Ruby was scuffing her feet, just a few movements short
of petulantly kicking at the ground like a sulky child. "I don't
see why you cannot trust to the police here to solve the
case."

Because I want my house back. Cordelia sighed.

"You saw the state of the local constable, did you not?

Now if this were London or Manchester, then perhaps I could believe that the perpetrator would be brought to justice. But here? Crimes are investigated when the victim pays enough for the prosecution. Do you not see that as a grave injustice? There is no family of this poor boy to pay for it."

"What of his mother?"

"I do not know." Cordelia stopped short and fished around in her bag. "And that is a mightily good point. Well. I am glad I brought you along; talking to you helps me see the correct questions to ask!"

"It was I that asked."

"Yes, yes, quite. And thank you." Cordelia scribbled in her notebook: *What of his mother?* "The father was a drunk, but I have not heard at all of any other family."

"So why are we going to the Post Office?"

"Why, you almost sound interested."

"Talking about is makes this tedious journey marginally less tedious."

"Ruby!"

"My lady."

"Huh. Well. Listen, and learn. And ... do feel free to

speak up with any insights. If they are relevant and helpful," Cordelia added in a warning tone.

"My lady," Ruby said again in that infuriatingly ambiguous tone.

"It's a curious thing," Cordelia said. She slowed her walking pace as she tried to organise her thoughts. "When I was last in the Post Office, the clerk told me of the letters that the doctor had sent to Liverpool. And the letters that Ewatt Carter-Hall had been sending abroad. I mentioned the fact of the doctor's letters to Mr Carter-Hall."

"Mm."

"When I saw Mr Carter-Hall last night, at the card game, he mentioned that he had evidence that the doctor had been married before, in Liverpool, and that he had killed his wife."

Ruby burst out laughing.

"Ruby!" Cordelia said in shock. "I have not spoken in jest."

"No, my lady, no. But does it not sound ridiculous to you? What evidence has Mr Carter-Hall seen? And why would he have sought it out? And why would he tell you and not the authorities?"

"I agree that all seems suspicious. And that is why we are going to the Post Office. For Mr Carter-Hall must have gone there after I spoke with him, and obtained some information from there; perhaps he saw a letter, or pursued it to its destination. I intend to get to the bottom of this."

* * *

She greeted the whiskery clerk jovially, and he remembered her. "What can I do for you today, my lady?" he said. Next to him, a boy was wrapping up a large and awkward parcel in brown paper. Two young women sat on wooden chairs, watching. And as soon as Cordelia began to talk to the clerk, a young man in a rather racy checked suit entered, and stood behind her to wait his turn to be served. Ruby went to the shop side of the building, and peered up at the shelves behind the counter there.

She leaned over the counter, trying to be discrete and not overheard. "I am wondering if I might speak to you further about those letters that the doctor sent to Liverpool."

"What letters? What was that? You wish to write to a doctor in Liverpool?"

She glanced to each side. Everyone was listening.

Of course. Everyone knew that this was the place to come for gossip, but it was unlikely that the clerk wanted to celebrate that fact so openly. "May we speak privately?"

He licked his lips nervously. "You may step into the back room. One moment. Charlie, see to the gentleman, if you will."

She followed him around the polished counter and through a simple door into a stockroom. He seemed embarrassed at its disorder. "My lady, I do apologise for the mess."

"It matters not. Now, these letters. I believe that Mr Ewatt Carter-Hall came and spoke with you about the content of those letters?"

"Ah ... no, no I am afraid I cannot recall."

"Oh, come now. It was but a few days ago."

"I must not divulge people's confidences," he said. "It would be entirely improper."

"Of course. I am not asking you to reveal the doctor's correspondence ... only what Mr Carter-Hall learned from it."

"But you see, that would be the same thing. No, my

lady, I cannot." He drew himself up and puffed out his chest, inflating his round body like a ball. "Now, if you please … I am a busy man."

Oh for goodness' sake. She could have shaken him in her infuriation. She stamped out of the shop, and was met outside by Ruby.

"I assume things went ill?"

"The wretched little man has had an ill-timed attack of conscience, and will not speak. I can surmise that Carter-Hall did, indeed, come and talk to him. But now he will not say further! Partly, that is because there are others present within earshot. Maybe he has been threatened. But I have a plan."

"Oh dear."

"Come, now. Enough of that. And I need your help."

"Oh dear!"

"Ruby. Where is your spirit of adventure? Life isn't all hiding in bushes with footmen, you know."

"That's exciting enough for me."

"Pfft. Now, here it is. We shall wait here until the Post Office is empty. Then you shall go in – yes, you! You have charms. You have that way about you. You know, a young woman's way. Go and speak in flattering terms to the clerk."

"And you?"

"I shall be outside, preventing anyone from entering to interrupt proceedings."

"Why, my lady, how far do you wish these proceedings to ... proceed?"

"Not *that* far," Cordelia said with a snap. "Keep your gloves on."

* * *

The moment came soon. The Post Office and the shop were briefly empty. Cordelia pushed Ruby into the Post Office and took up her position at the door, standing tall and firm with a Valkyrie air about her. She had her back to the door and looked out onto the street, daring anyone to approach.

One minute passed. Then the door jangled and Ruby cannoned into her from behind, sending Cordelia stepping forward and almost into the path of a passing carriage.

"I am afraid I have had no luck," Ruby said. "Also, he called me a cheeky minx. And other things."

"Did he, indeed?" Cordelia glared at the door. Slandering her servant was akin to slandering *herself* and it would not do. "I shall see about that–"

She grabbed the handle and began to push the door open, inwards, but Ruby laid a hand on her arm. Her grip was firm, and it was most unexpected.

That her servant might presume to do such a thing stopped Cordelia short. She had the door half-open, and one foot over the threshold. She looked down at Ruby's hand.

Ruby did not remove it. "My lady," she said forcefully. "It would be better left alone."

Cordelia wrenched her hand free of both the door handle and Ruby's grasp. She began to walk back to Hugo's estate, very quickly and very angrily indeed.

Something had changed.

Something unsettling.

The maid had laid a hand on her.

She had not said anything.

When she reached the edge of Hugo's grounds, Geoffrey was loitering by the stone pillars, as if looking out for her. He stepped forward but she was in no mood for his arrogant and unbecoming paternalism. He, too, was overstepping his bounds. She swept past him, her head held high, heading defiantly for Hugo's wine cellar. She needed to make plans. She needed a drink.

Ruby stayed behind, lingering, to talk to him in a hushed voice.

CHAPTER EIGHTEEN

I am a stupid silly woman with stupid silly ideas. Cordelia burped, giggled, and then felt a threatening uprising of tears. She blinked them back.

She was sitting on the back stairs of Wallerton Manor, hunched up in semi-darkness, leaning heavily against the cold wall. Her feet were tucked up on the step below, and she clutched a bottle of whisky to her stomach. It would have been chilly where she sat, but the alcohol was keeping her warm.

She'd intended to have a small glass while she went through her notes. She had a mission. She *had* to win Clarfields back.

But somewhere along the line, the alcohol had entered into league with her usually-suppressed self-doubt, and now she was here, far too gone in her cups to think straight, and realising she'd made a terrible mistake.

If I thought I was the laughing stock of society after my failed book of manners, she thought fuzzily, *what will they make of me now! For Hugo will not keep this folly to himself, will he? Oh no. Indeed, he will use it to bring me so low that I have no choice but to marry him. He will win – and he won't stop there.*

For a man who can be pleasant company, he is one horrible person.

There was a scratching in the wainscot, and she tensed, her drink-befuddled senses suddenly alert. It must have been a mouse, for the skittering faded.

Then a wave of light flooded the floor at the bottom of the stairs. These steps were the servants' access, and did not merit carpeting, and the hard floor shone, reflecting the lamp light. A figure stepped forward, merely a dark shape behind the lamp it carried.

"My lady." It was the gruff voice of Geoffrey.

And behind him came Ruby. "My lady, Claire told us you were here."

"Who's Claire?"

"One of the under-kitchen-maids."

"Hugo has too many staff."

"You've had too much to drink," Geoffrey said, climbing the stairs to her. He set the lamp a few steps above them, and angled it so as not to dazzle. "Stanley, come you up here."

The angular lad clambered up the stairs, his rough boots clattering, and he thrust out a cloth-wrapped parcel.

Geoffrey took it and unwrapped it on the step between them. "Mrs Unsworth bakes a good loaf, whatever else you might say of the woman."

"I am here, you know," the cook snapped from the darkness below.

"Good, then take the compliment. And that cheese you were after, well, it's arrived, at last. So here you are." He cut off a hunk of cheese and laid it inelegantly on a slab of thick bread.

The rich scent of the blued cheese seemed to hit Cordelia between the eyes. As she reached for it, Geoffrey deftly leaned in and took the bottle of whisky from her. She nearly dropped the bread in her effort to claw back the bottle, but in the end, the lure of the new cheese won out.

Geoffrey bent down and passed the bottle via Stanley to Ruby, who disappeared. She returned very quickly with a large mug. That was relayed up to Cordelia, who was surprised to find it was hot coffee.

"I am not drunk," she protested.

"You missed dinner," Ruby said. "Our suite is full of bottles. You smell. And you're hiding on the stairs. So…"

"It's all gone wrong," Cordelia said. *I fear I have lost Clarfields. And I have lost you all your jobs and positions. How can I tell you?*

"Whisky does that," Ruby said. "Wine or some sherry, that would have been better."

"Now listen," Geoffrey said. "You drink that down yourself, and let me tell you something."

She braced herself for an inappropriate lecture.

But he surprised her. "Ruby here, mistress tattle-tale that she is, and you ought to thank her for it, well, Ruby here told me of your dealings at the Post Office, and how that man slighted you."

"Oh."

"And so I took a walk down there myself," Geoffrey continued. "And I had a little chat with the clerk, and persuaded him of the error of his ways."

"Oh … no." The half-giggles, half-sobs, rose up again.

"Do not worry," Geoffrey said, lightly. "No bones were actually broken."

Such a statement had the effect of sobering Cordelia up far quicker than coffee and stinky cheese. "I am glad to hear it," she murmured weakly. She didn't want to probe the alternate interpretations of the sentence.

"I would have had a hard time of it anyway," Geoffrey said cheerfully. "I mean, finding those bones under all that fat, eh! First, I would have needed to have taken a stout stick to the man..."

"Geoffrey! Please."

"As you wish. Tis only the same as tenderising meat. Anyways, the outcome of this was, that he was minded to reveal a few things to me, as he ought to have done to you, and saved himself the bother of – of being persuaded by me, as it were. To wit, that Ewatt Carter-Hall *did* speak to him on the matter of the letters that were sent to Liverpool. And that the same gentleman *did* then send his own letters to Liverpool, and received replies thereof. And he warned the clerk to say nothing more of the matter. Until I came along, that is." Geoffrey snickered in a low grumbling way.

"But what was contained in those letters?"

"He could not rightly say. He does not read other folks' communications, so he says, and I do believe him."

"Then all was for naught."

"Not so. For one reply was a telegram, and it went to Cambridge and thence came here written on a card. So no secrecy was possible. And it confirmed the date and place of Doctor Donald Arnall's marriage … to a Miss Clara Fellowes. Clara. And that Mrs Clara Arnall is, indeed, dead. And that the sender would be very grateful for the known whereabouts of Mrs Clara Arnall's husband so that – in his words – 'matters may at last be settled.' So, there you are!"

Cordelia sipped at the coffee and struggled to make sense of what she had heard.

"What does it all mean?" she said weakly.

Geoffrey looked down the stairs at Ruby. Cordelia followed his gaze. The shadowy figures of Mrs Unsworth and Stanley were still there, too.

"Does it have to mean anything?" Mrs Unsworth snapped.

"A death does. We both know that. A murder does, in particular. The murder of a boy, alone and unmourned." *It could mean keeping my home. Our home.*

"He was not a boy," Mrs Unsworth said.

"Everyone talks about him like he was not yet a man. He lived alone. Had he a sweetheart? We know nothing about him. Except that someone disliked him enough to seek him out and kill him."

"Mrs Hurrell—"

"I do not believe she did it," Cordelia said. "I am convinced of it."

"Then it would be a grave injustice indeed, for I fear she is to hang for it," Geoffrey said. "That is the latest talk."

Cordelia felt the chill begin to creep up her legs. She wrapped her hands around the now-empty coffee mug. "And there is another question that I have, about the doctor. What does Ewatt Carter-Hall have so badly against Doctor Donald Arnall? They will not call him for their sick child. He seeks information to defame him. He hopes to pin the murder on him."

"*Pin* it? What if it is true, and the doctor is the culprit?" Ruby said.

"Maybe that is the case. But I am suspicious of them all. Not a single one of them is telling the whole truth," Cordelia said bitterly. "I want to know what they all hide.

And it seems to me very strange that no one in this town likes the doctor – yet he seems a perfectly pleasant man to me."

"Do they tell you they dislike him?" Geoffrey asked.

"They talk of him … strangely. They mistrust him." Cordelia nodded down the stairs. "As Ruby can attest to."

"It is true. He is keen to help the poor and he is full of new ideas. And maybe that's the problem," Ruby added. "He is not local and he is not traditional."

"Could it just be that?" Cordelia wondered. "I ask again … what does Carter-Hall have against the doctor that he would dig up the matter of his previous wife?"

Stanley spoke at last, his voice rasping in the darkness. Perhaps it was easier for him to talk when he could not see his mistress clearly, for his stammer was diminished. "M-maybe Mr Carter-Hall did so because it was the right thing to do."

Ruby turned on him before Cordelia could speak. "The right thing to do? Listen to you, stammering-boy. Carter-Hall might be lying for all we know. He could be setting the doctor up."

"Again, for what ends?" Cordelia said. "It seems too

elaborate to me."

"Anyway," Mrs Unsworth said, "As for me, I don't reckon as the ends justify the means. That Carter-Hall, didn't he sneak around and read letters or threaten the post master or somesuch? I can't rightly follow it, but I don't know that doing wrong to find out what is right can be justified. Not even in your churchy world, Stanley."

"God's laws t-t-trump man's," Stanley said.

"Oh, get you!" Ruby said. "You speak up louder when you're angry. Go on, get passionate about something. Let's hear you give us some fire and brimstone."

"Tisn't to be m-mocked about," he said, but his stammer had immediately grown worse, and Ruby laughed cruelly.

Cordelia thought that she had been forgotten about as the servants teased and taunted one another, but Mrs Unsworth stepped in, hissing, "Hush, you all. Not in front of the mistress!"

Everything went silent.

Geoffrey reached out and took the empty mug from her unresisting hands. She sighed and straightened up, feeling sick.

Mrs Unsworth whispered something that Cordelia couldn't hear, and the figures at the bottom of the stairs melted backwards, swallowed by the dark. The spell was broken. Geoffrey got to his feet and extended his free hand, but Cordelia ignored it. She got up, unsteadily.

"Thank you for your kindnesses," she said, hearing an ungracious note in her voice, and hating herself for it. "I shall retire."

"Shall I send Ruby to attend to you?"

"No. She is free for what remains of the evening."

"As you wish."

She gathered up her skirt and ploughed her way up the narrow stairs, feeling along the corridor at the top so that she could come out through a servant's door and into the main house once more.

She could sense Geoffrey still on the stairs, watching and listening to her leave.

* * *

Cordelia felt restless and alone, and annoyed with herself for having had a moment of weakness – and one that was witnessed by her staff, no less! She shook herself all over, like a dog leaving a river, and sat down on her bed. She would have to undress herself, and see to her toilette, but now the alcohol was wearing off, she was steadier on her feet. She set about the task wearily.

Once she was dressed in her long nightgown, her hair neatly done about her head, she pulled a leather notebook from a drawer and slithered onto the bed, tucking the pillows up behind her to make a comfortable rest for her back.

The notebook contained a random mess of quotes and half-remembered poems, significant sayings, sketches and lists.

She flicked to the list that had pride of place on the back page.

At the top, in her scrawling copperplate, she had written PROJECTS and underlined it many times.

Below that, in smaller letters and much scratched through, was written "Compile a modern book of manners."

Well, that had ended badly.

There was also, "Write a blistering romance about an army colonel and his long-lost sweetheart who now lives in seclusion in the woods." Why had she thought that would ever appeal to anyone? She had grown bored of writing it by page twelve, but had ploughed on in increasing irritation until she had given up and killed both the hero and the heroine in an unexpected train derailment somewhere around chapter seven.

"Write a natural history of the hedgerow plants of Berkshire." That had sold a handful of copies. It was a shame that she had had hundreds printed, however.

At the bottom was her latest idea. "Write a series of articles that will develop into books exploring the regional cookery of the British Isles."

It still excited her, and gave her a reason to travel. But now she drew a line through that, too, and wrote, "Find the person who murdered Thomas Bains and bring them to justice. Thereby saving my house. And escaping Hugo."

It was as ludicrous an idea as any of the others.

And yet, in all this, that poor man lies unmourned and his life is finished before it even began. She felt a flicker of anger deep inside. She folded the book closed and put it on her bedside table, and extinguished her lamp. She fought the pillows for a moment before she was comfortable, and lay down.

The anger remained. She burned with it all.

She shot upright in bed when she heard the outer door to her suite click open and closed, and light footsteps shuffle across the carpeted rooms.

"Ruby?" she hissed, groping sideways in the dark for a heavy candlestick.

The door opened and pale yellow light edged the furniture. "Yes, my lady. Are you quite all right? May I get you anything?"

"Come here, girl. Ruby."

She came, setting one tall, wide candle on the bedside table, and stood next to the bed, her hands folded neatly in front of her body, looking every inch the biddable servant.

Cordelia felt the distance between them was an ocean. She patted the bed. "Sit."

Ruby wavered. "My lady, perhaps the alcohol still—"

"Sit!" She lowered her voice, and said, "I am sorry. Please, Ruby, sit with me. I am ... alone, and afraid."

That was enough to startle the maid. "You, my lady? Afraid?" She hitched her skirts and gingerly slipped onto the edge of the broad bed, moving the notebook that still lay in the rumbled bedclothes. She held it in her hands, unseeing, keeping her attention on her mistress.

"I must tell you something, Ruby," Cordelia said. "I am so sorry. This will shock you. It's not a tale of stallions or strange predilections. This is a matter of our futures. Together."

Ruby listened. Cordelia explained herself, and then explained herself again in different words, talking it over and over, just to get it straight in her own mind.

On her third attempt, Ruby stopped her, placing her small hand on Cordelia's wrist. The touch was another step across the ocean that separated them. "My lady," she said. "I have it. And I think we all knew that there was more to you, earlier this evening. Mrs Unsworth said as much though I ignored her."

"You mustn't ignore her," Cordelia said. "Except when she is being spiteful."

"Well, that is all of the time. But she said that something burned you deep, and now I know."

"And what do you think?"

Ruby laughed. "We do it!"

"We?"

Ruby still held the notebook in her free hand. She

tapped Cordelia's knee with it. "For certain, my lady, this is not a journey you can do alone. Anyway, it is to all of our benefit, is it not?"

"It is."

"So when do we start?"

"Tomorrow."

"And where do we start?"

Cordelia took the notebook from Ruby, and opened it at the last page she had been writing before she tried to sleep. "With Doctor Arnall? With the post office clerk? With Ewatt Carter-Hall? No," she said, decisively. "At the house of Mrs Hurrell. And in particular, I wish to know why she was so upset at the thought of anyone opening that drawer in her sideboard."

CHAPTER NINETEEN

"One night of drinking, I can cope with," Cordelia moaned as she sat in her dressing robe. She didn't dare to glance at herself in the looking-glass. She closed her eyes and let Ruby attend to her hair. "But two nights together … ah, I am getting old."

"It was not just two nights. There was a full day of drinking too. Anyway, I'm sure it's nothing that Mr Peeble's Salts can't cure," Ruby said breezily.

"Are you mocking me?"

"Me, my lady?"

"Hmm."

"Shall I call for breakfast to be served in your day room?"

"No. Let me dress; in my readings and research I came across a cure I wish to try. I need to visit the kitchens."

"Soot?"

"Please, Mrs Unsworth. I simply need a spoonful of the ashes from the fireplace. And some warm milk."

Mrs Unsworth's flabby face contorted, her mouth pulling down at the sides, making folds and creases in her cheeks. "Raw egg and vinegar, that is what you need, begging pardon."

"That has never worked for me. I should like to try this new medicine."

Cordelia sat at the large scrubbed table. It was the lull between breakfast and luncheon, and the maids were going quietly and calmly about their tasks. It didn't take as much to prepare the midday meal of cold meats and platters, and they conserved their energies for the hectic rush of later in the day. The other members of staff – those not employed in the kitchen – were all about their business as usual.

Except for Ralph Goody, the gardener, who had come into the kitchen with a box of freshly-dug vegetables.

"Hold – don't be taking them into the scullery before

I have seen to them," Mrs Unsworth ordered.

Ralph met Cordelia's eyes but quickly dropped his gaze. He looked uncomfortable at the intrusion of the lady into the servants' domain. It was not done. "Where is Mrs Kendal?" he asked, referring to the manor's cook.

"She is talking to Mr Hawke upstairs about the menu for the next few days." Mrs Unsworth got down on her knees and scraped at the side of the fire below the range, pulling forward some ash, and spreading it on a pan to cool. She moved about the kitchen as if it were her own.

"Of course." He stood to one side and waited as Mrs Unsworth heaved herself to her feet and showed Cordelia the ash. "Does this suffice?"

"It does. Tip it into the milk and warm it gently, and then I shall drink it."

Mrs Unsworth shook her head almost imperceptibly, but she did as she was told. She stood by the top of the range and stirred the pan. A chalky-sweet aroma filled the air.

"Where's Ruby?" Cordelia asked suddenly.

Mrs Unsworth shrugged, and bellowed, "Ruby!"

The maid popped her head into the kitchen. "I was

looking for the cheese you had ordered in," she said. "That blue. And the other. Which store was it in? I have searched them all, I am sure of it."

"It was in the store by the dairy, on a high shelf," Mrs Unsworth said. She poured the grey liquid into a glass, and handed it to Cordelia. There were disconcerting lumps floating in it.

"It's not there now," Ruby insisted.

"I am not surprised," Mrs Unsworth said. "Two days ago, a wheel of cheddar went missing, too. And yesterday I could not find the pigeon pie I had made. Goody, you have a thief on the premises ... ah, but you knew that already, did you not?"

Ralph shook his head vehemently. "No, not at all. For certain, we *did* have a thief," he said, blinking briefly at Cordelia. "But it was Thomas Bains, and now he is dead, so there is no more thievery here. Upon my life, no, there is not. Just over-addled women."

Mrs Unsworth folded her arms. "There is still a problem here, and I do not know why no one does anything."

"Madam! I can assure you there ain't no problem here, and if there were, we should see to it."

"And I can assure you that you *do* have a problem, and if you people weren't so lazy and up your own–"

"Mrs Unsworth!" Cordelia barked, and the woman stopped, her mouth snapping shut. She glared at Ralph.

He muttered, "Visitors here ought to be mindful of their *place*," and left sharply.

Cordelia did not think the remark was aimed entirely at Mrs Unsworth.

She sipped at the drink. It was utterly revolting. She made an effort to drink it down while it was still warm, but when her teeth closed on some gritty particles, she nearly brought it back up again. She forced another mouthful down, and then gave up. "Thank you for this," she said grimly. "I fear it might not catch on."

"Shall I fetch some eggs?" Ruby asked.

"Good lord, no. That would be adding insult to injury," Cordelia said. *Soot, milk and then raw egg …* she swallowed. "A cup of tea would suffice."

"Perhaps we ought to consult the doctor," Ruby said. "And it would give you an excuse to speak to him."

Cordelia shook her head. "I am not yet at the stage of talking to the doctor because I cannot handle my drink," she said. "Today, we must visit Mrs Hurrell's cottage, yes. But I was thinking about him – the doctor – again this morning. We had been talking of the connection between the doctor and Carter-Hall, but what of the other connection?"

"Between...?"

"Between Doctor Arnall, and Thomas Bains," Cordelia said.

Ruby shrugged, and Cordelia sighed in frustration. Ruby chewed her lip for a moment, and then went to the door that led to the scullery. "Claire. Is Rose in the dairy?"

There was a muffled conversation and then two maids entered behind Ruby. "My lady, this is Claire and this is Rose."

Both girls bobbed, eyes on the floor. Rose's cheeks were as pink as her chapped hands. Claire was a scrawny thing, with prominent blue veins in her temples and along the backs of her wiry hands.

"You both knew Thomas Bains, did you not?" Ruby said.

Cordelia opened her mouth to say something but Ruby shot her a look, and she remained silent. She suddenly realised that the girls would talk to Ruby far more willingly than they would speak to Cordelia herself.

"We did," Claire said. She might be the smaller of the two, but she stood upright and spoke boldly.

"Who did he argue with?"

Both girls stifled their giggles. "Everyone," Claire said. "He worked here, on and off, and he was forever arguing with Mr Goody, you know, the head gardener. Proper humdingers and all."

"What about the doctor?"

Claire shook her head but looked at Rose, who was frowning. "He did, yes. Do you not remember, Claire? He came in here, Thomas, in a fearful strop, because he said that the doctor would not see him."

"I cannot believe that!" Cordelia said, unable to stop herself.

The girls clammed up immediately, and shrank in on themselves.

"I am sorry, I am sorry; ignore me," Cordelia said hastily. "I do not mean to say that I do not believe you. I do. Please. Carry on. I will be silent."

With a little chiding and probing from Ruby, the maids

began to open up again.

"I think I do remember," Claire said, looking intently at Rose for confirmation. "Though it is hard to separate out all the rants and arguments that Thomas had. Yet I am not sure he was ill."

Rose nodded. "He did not look ill, and he was never a sickly type of person. But he came in here and he broke that jug. That's why I remember. I had to sweep it up, and when I was doing so, Mrs Kendal came in, and she began to blame me until I could explain, and I am sure she still thinks I lied."

"Oh, she would."

Ruby said, "Did Thomas say why the doctor would not see him? Was he busy, perhaps?"

"I do not think so," Rose said. "He could not account for it, and he seemed most put out."

The two maids shrugged, then, their information exhausted. Cordelia thanked them both profusely, and released them back to their tasks. She rubbed her face, massaging her temples in slow circles to ease her headache.

"It might be something and it might be nothing, my lady," Ruby said.

"Indeed," Cordelia said. "But I do think something is strange here; in this house and in this town. And I declare to you now, Ruby, that we shall get to the bottom of it. What say you?"

Ruby folded her arms, and leaned back against the wall. She smiled. "I think that you are right," she said. "Not for Stanley's reasoning, though. He will do only what is morally correct. As for me…"

"Yes?"

Ruby's smile became a grin. "I fancy some adventure, my lady. Don't you?"

"Oh yes."

Mrs Unsworth tutted loudly and began to turn away. Cordelia stopped her, saying, "And do not think you are not part of this, Mrs Unsworth."

"I cannot see what part I might have to play here."

"Indeed, Mrs Unsworth, you have a vital task only this day. For I need to visit the good doctor's wife later this afternoon, and I shall not go empty-handed. A pie, I think. A deep game pie. That will do nicely."

Mrs Unsworth muttered and stamped out of the kitchen, heading to the stores to look for suitable meat.

Ruby and Cordelia's eyes met.

"The adventure begins."

CHAPTER TWENTY

Cordelia and Ruby walked to the small town, and went over what they already knew about Mrs Hurrell, each one finishing the other's sentences.

"So she ran a disorderly house in London–"

"Eight years ago, is that right?"

"Eight years," Cordelia confirmed. "But here, she is a law-abiding landlady."

"So," Ruby said, "she used her profits from her previous business?"

"Undoubtedly. But she has not been accepted. Her neighbour, Mrs Kale, did not care for her."

"Did Mrs Kale strike you as a woman that would care for anyone? What was she, a laundress?"

"True," Cordelia said. "That line of work would make anyone a bitter sort, I think."

"Undoubtedly," Ruby echoed, and laughed. As they turned down the side street that the cottage lay on, she asked, "And what do we look for, here? Was there not a note?"

"Of course! She claimed that she was out of the house because she had been sent a note. Well, we must find it. And we must see what she wished to hide in that sideboard of hers."

They paused outside the house. It was mid-morning. There were no men to be seen or heard; all would be away at work. Work continued here, too, of another sort. Very young children ran in and out of the houses. A few older children, those who could not find employment, were engaged in looking after the younger ones, or set to household tasks. And Cordelia knew, as she looked at the doors and windows, that within were the women, washing and sewing and mending and cooking and cleaning.

Cordelia knocked very lightly on the door, and then pushed it open to peer inside.

"Well, this is not London," she said. "There, this space would have been inhabited again within days, if not hours."

They stepped inside, leaving the door open as far as

possible. It was not only to let the light in. There was a desperate need to let the smell out.

Ruby pulled a handkerchief from her small bag, and held it to her nose. Cordelia let her eyes adjust, and said, "I do not think it is anything more sinister than some leftover food, and dust, and a lack of air."

"And an unemptied chamberpot," Ruby gasped.

"Oh. Yes, and that. Try not to think about it. You'll only make it worse."

Cordelia breathed as lightly as she could and went to the sideboard. It was a dark wood thing, well-made and once very expensive. It was a strange thing to see in an otherwise poor dwelling, but then, furniture such as this would be treasured and passed on. She pulled open the drawer that Mrs Hurrell had been so keen to keep shut.

Ruby came to her side. "What is it?"

"Newspapers." Cordelia pulled the yellowing sheets out and piled them on the sideboard. She felt around in the drawer, and then dragged the whole thing free. It was nothing but an empty box, and there were no secret panels or hidden notes.

"Just newspapers." Ruby looked at them. "And not

recent, nor local. These are the London papers from some years ago."

The text on the large sheets was dense and ran in many columns. The front pages were given over to advertisements – an auction, a new hair perfume, sanitary corsets – and Cordelia skimmed over that. She turned to the scant inner pages.

There was a rant from a Church of England minister. A supposedly witty analysis of the current season by a smug and anonymous "observer." Some political commentary that would have been as appropriate ten years ago as one year ago. *Ever thus,* she thought.

A name caught her eye. "Ruby, look here." She laid her finger on the paper. "Mr Carter-Hall."

"Oho?" They craned their heads to read, squinting in the gloom of the cottage.

"It's something and nothing," Cordelia said at last.

"It's everything," Ruby said. "His bank had gone bust!"

"But that is business. Look at the date of the paper; it is a few years old. His new venture is going well."

"Is it? His staff leave. His house is in disarray."

"I concede that," Cordelia said. "But maybe he is

ploughing his money into tiding his business through a bad time, though when we spoke of it, he seemed very happy."

"He would *seem* so because if he did not, no one would invest, would they?"

"But what is all this to Mrs Hurrell? Why would she be concerned with the doings of a bank, some time ago?" Cordelia scanned through the rest of the paper. A woman had been sentenced to six month's hard labour for keeping a disorderly house, and for a moment she thought she had it; but the woman was called Theresa Juliette, and did not match Mrs Hurrell's description, especially considering that the offender was French.

Ruby moved away, leafing through the detritus on the rickety table. "What of this note that she was supposed to have received?"

Cordelia followed, and together they searched the room.

"Nothing."

"Perhaps she lied."

"Or perhaps," Cordelia said, pointing to the dead range, "it was disposed of."

They both studied the ash. "There is no way of

knowing," Ruby said. "But I can collect it for you."

"Why, am I a chemist now?"

"No, I mean for your hangovers, in case you wish to drink it."

"Hush."

"Looters is it?"

At the sound of the harsh voice, Cordelia and Ruby both whirled around to face the figure that had appeared in the doorway. "Looters, on my word!"

"Mrs Kale." Cordelia stepped forward and affected her most upper-class tone. "How delightful to make your acquaintance once more. And how do you do today?"

"How do I do what?"

"You. Do you."

"I don't. What do you want?"

Cordelia smiled. "You."

Mrs Kale took a half-step back but then drew herself up tall. "I am innocent."

"Of course you are," Cordelia said. "Come now. A strong woman like yourself need fear no one. Tell me about the day of the murder."

"Why?"

"Because I imagine that no one else has asked you that, have they? They don't know, these constables and magistrates and the like. They don't realise what information women like you have. What power, indeed. I am asking you because no one else has thought to."

Was it enough? It seemed so. Mrs Kale inflated her chest and allowed herself a short moment of preening. She said, "I don't rightly know what to say. I heard the noise and I come on through, and found her like that, against the wall, crying."

"Tell me what noise you heard, exactly."

"I figures that I heard the noise of the fighting tween them. I ignored it. There's no call for anyone to go poking into another's business. I heard him, that Thomas, shout something. There was a thump. Then, nothing for a long while so I got on with my work until I realised she was crying and wailing."

Ruby plucked at Cordelia's sleeve. "Nothing for a long while," she whispered.

"Yes. Mrs Kale, what did Thomas shout?"

"I don't know. Something along the lines of, *you have no care for those who will be … ruined by your actions.* And then he said he was going to go to someone, but I didn't hear any more, really. And I might be wrong."

"I am sure you are not. Is there anything else you can remember?"

"No."

"Thank you," Cordelia said. As she moved towards the door, Ruby spoke up.

"Mrs Kale, begging pardon, did Mr Carter-Hall and Mrs Hurrell know one another?"

Mrs Kale shrugged. "No, of course not. As long as he got the rent off her through his bailiffs then why would he want to get to know her?"

* * *

A game pie is not a swift thing to cook and cool. Late that afternoon, it was finally in a fit state to be transported. Cordelia left Ruby behind to attend to some mending, with additional instructions to "have a good think." There had been no sign of Hugo all day, now; she wondered if he was regretting his wager.

She asked Geoffrey to drive her to the doctor's house,

hoping that the hour of her visit was not too anti-social. Certainly they seemed to keep to less strict hours in the countryside, and she was hopeful she would be received.

The doctor's house was a new building, with large airy windows either side of a smart white door. The size of the windows, she thought, meant he could get away with having fewer overall, and avoid the higher rates of window tax. There was a neatly clipped privet hedge at the front of the house, and an archway to the side that led to the stable at the back. Of course, a country doctor would have need of his own horses. Geoffrey pulled up outside the front door, and by the time she was standing on the gravel with the pie in her hands, the staff in the house had noticed her arrival and the front door was standing open.

It was a woman, a smartly dressed housekeeper, who descended the steps to welcome her. She had one of those young-old faces, with bright eyes set deep in a sea of wrinkles yet her teeth were white and her smile warm.

"Is Mrs Arnall at home?" Cordelia asked, and introduced herself.

"She is. Please do step inside." The housekeeper nodded at Geoffrey. "If you go through to the side, you will find refreshments with our Bill."

As soon as Cordelia stepped into the hallway, she was met by none other than Doctor Donald Arnall himself. He looked surprised, and well he might, as he was shockingly undressed in nothing but a pair of trousers and a white shirt.

This was not the time to giggle and flutter and panic. Cordelia's good breeding took over. She kept her eyes firmly on his face, and smiled. "Good afternoon, sir. I am hoping to meet your good lady wife. I am assured that she is at home."

"And you've brought a pie!" he exclaimed, as if he wasn't nearly naked in his jacketless state.

"My cook is a marvel," she said. "It is game pie."

"I thank you. Mrs Lyall, will you take it to the kitchens? Forgive us. We do not eat too much meat here, but I assure you that it will not go to waste."

The man was impossible. He was standing there, continuing the conversation as if it were a perfectly normal situation. Was it some kind of test? She would match him, she vowed. "Is meat not essential to a healthy life?" she said.

"In moderation, yes, but there are different kinds of

meat, and of course, different methods of preparation that affect the digestibility of it. As a man of science, I am committed to exploring these matters. And it is my fervent belief that what ails a man most, these days, is the consumption of too much red meat over the more healthful and life-giving properties to be found in vegetables."

She had been trained to maintain a socially acceptable conversation in almost any topic, but talking at length about vegetables was tasking, even for her. "How interesting," she said, stalling for time. What on earth could she ask about vegetables?

There was a light in the doctor's eyes. She had not had the chance to converse with him for so long a time, and so close up. He was not smiling, but when he spoke, she knew he was teasing her. "Interesting? Even I do not find vegetables themselves to be of high interest, but their effects – ah, now that is the fascination. Come now. We can discuss potatoes, or we can seek out Hetty."

She handed the pie over to the waiting housekeeper, and followed Doctor Arnall through a wide set of double doors. As she was behind him now, she could steal a glance at his body; he was lean and lithe and walked like a racehorse.

She jerked her gaze upright as they came upon his wife, who was sitting by the window and reading a book. She had been so absorbed in it that she had not heard them enter the room. There was a flurry of introductions, and then mercifully the doctor left. Cordelia hoped it was to dress properly. The man was in sore need of a few more layers upon him.

Mrs Arnall put her book to one side and rose. Like her husband, she was lean and slender, with warm brown eyes and an unfussy way of dressing her hair. Cordelia wanted to like her immediately.

"Dear Lady Cornbrook, how nice of you to come and see me."

"I thought it was about time," Cordelia said. On an impulse, she said, "Do call me Cordelia."

"And I must be Hetty to you," she replied. "Come. Shall we take tea in the garden?"

In stark contrast to the slovenly nature of Freda Carter-Hall's reception, by the time that Cordelia and Hetty were seated on ornate ironwork chairs, there was upon a table, a tray with all manner of good things to eat, some cool glasses of iced lemon-water, and a steaming hot pot of tea as well. But there was something odd about the scones.

"What is the secret to this?" Cordelia asked as she lifted the brown scone to examine it. "For I must confess I am interested in all the culinary arts…"

"We use the whole part of the grain in the flour," Hetty explained. "I know that some will say it's only fit for the poor, and horses, but we find that it aids the stomach wonderfully."

"Oh. Indeed." Cordelia had never had to eat anything other than the finest milled white flour, and she bit into the new scone with curiosity. It was chewy. But not, on second thoughts, too bad, considering.

Hetty smiled. "I know. Our ideas are considered most outlandish here. Why, in London, Donald could bathe with quite a crowd in the Serpentine but here, he is restricted to sneaking around at quiet times of the day, just to be able to take a dip in the river!"

Why anyone should want to dip anything, let alone their own body, in the local weed-strewn rivers was a mystery. Cordelia hoped that her grimace was hidden by the scone as she lifted it to her mouth.

"Did you live in London before you came here?"

Cordelia asked.

"Briefly. You must try our bread," she urged. She pointed to the standard long thin cucumber sandwiches, although the cook had neglected to cut the crusts off. *Perhaps it was deliberate*, Cordelia thought.

"Thank you. Yes, it is good. And before London?" she said, angling for more information.

"The north west. But Donald is forever seeking more information, more data, more knowledge. That is why we move so often," she said.

Oh, really? "And have you been married long?"

"Oh, you mean to ask, where are our children?" Hetty said, blushing. It was not at all what Cordelia meant but she nodded anyway. "We have not yet been blessed," Hetty went on. "But all in good time, I am sure."

"I am sure." Cordelia accepted a cup of tea that Hetty stood to pour. She was thinking of a question to frame about the north west - specifically, where did they live, and when. But she did not get the chance. As Hetty sat down again, she leaned in and dropped her voice.

"Now, did you hear the latest news regarding the dreadful murder?" she asked.

"I did not. What has happened?" Cordelia was immediately alert. Was she about to be fed more lies by the murderer's accomplice?

"Mrs Hurrell, the primary suspect – indeed, the only suspect – has been released!"

Cordelia gaped for a moment. She had not expected that revelation. The last she had heard, Mrs Hurrell was to be hung. She sipped at her tea to churn things over in her mind. At last, she said, "You say the only suspect. Is there no one else to be considered, do you know?"

"I have not heard so. I believe they are now accounting it the work of a passing madman, perhaps, and the authorities intend to close the case. And what is more – I also heard that your information was highly valuable to them! Yes, they considered your words carefully. Your conclusions about the way the murderer must have escaped were well-regarded."

"Oh, really?" She could not help but preen a little at that. Was it enough to win the wager? Not if no one was brought to account – damn them! She was only just getting started. She bit down the feeling of being betrayed. "Goodness."

"You should have made a fine lady-constable," Hetty said.

"Is there even such a thing?"

"Of course not." They both laughed at the absurdity of it, but Hetty then said, "Though one would think that a woman might do a fine job of it. Oh, no, not the grappling with criminals in the streets, of course. But in other matters, those of the mind. More delicate matters, that call for careful watching and questioning. I think we might do mightily well in such things."

Cordelia nodded, trying not to let the thrill she felt show on her face. Hetty was right, she was so right; and it seemed like a confirming sign from the universe that this was the topic of conversation.

She wanted to spill all her secret hopes and dreams, then, and indeed she might have done, but there was a commotion by the doors that led out onto the terrace where they presently sat.

"Hetty! Oh, and Corde-e-e-lia!" The manic, frazzled figure of Freda Carter-Hall appeared, closely followed by the frowning housekeeper.

Hetty rose, and waved the housekeeper away. "Ah,

Freda, how lovely to see you."

Cordelia remained sitting, and folded her hands in her lap, observing. The woman was full of energy, a suspicious amount of energy to be sure; it was not morphia that sizzled in her eyes this day.

"And that woman of yours said you were not at home!" Freda said, descending on them. She flung herself into a chair but rather than coming to rest, she fiddled and twisted her hands, she kicked her feet and she looked about relentlessly. "But I knew. Oh yes. I saw your carriage, Cordelia, and so I knew that Hetty was here and receiving guests. I am clever like that, you know! I see everything," she added in a low whisper.

"Do you, indeed?" Cordelia said drily. "Did you see the murderer of Thomas Bains?"

"Who? Oh! That boy. That is yesterday's news. Do you know, I had quite forgotten about it. No, the talk now is all about Brazil!"

Freda began to talk at length about a distant cousin of hers, a man of some renown who was a high-placed officer in the Royal Navy, and his escapades at sea now that the Act was finally passed which authorised the interception of slave vessels from Brazil. Cordelia noted that Freda's excitement was not aimed at the moral or ethical debates about the Act, but instead the fact that her cousin had been injured and was *awfully* brave and *terribly* stoical and *dreadfully* mangled about the face and *whatever was to become of his poor wife* and so on and so forth.

Hetty interrupted the wearingly flow of words with the question that Cordelia wanted to ask: "And how is your husband?"

Freda pulled at a long thread of her skirts and it did not break; ominously, it kept on unravelling. "Oh, he is in Bristol. No, London. Somewhere. He is gone to London – or wherever – on some awfully, awfully important bank business. I do not understand how a bank can have so much business that needs attending to. Though I daresay, there are his other *interests* there which occupy much of his time." She was no longer giggling. Her mouth was ugly in a down-turned sneer.

"Has he other businesses aside from banking?" Cordelia asked. Hetty shot her a warning look, but Cordelia pretended not to notice.

"In a manner of speaking. It is the way of men, is it

not? I have a fancy to take a lover myself!" Freda suddenly declared, jumping to her feet and startling both Cordelia and Hetty. She began to twirl across the terrace, somewhat clumsily. "A fine, strong man who will whisk me off my feet and take me to new places. France! Paris – yes, I should very much like to go to Paris, and there he will feed me the finest truffles and we shall dance all night."

Hetty was shaking her head. *So*, Cordelia thought, *it is as I suspected; Ewatt has many women. But I am slightly surprised that she is talking about it so freely. I suppose she must know that everyone knows...*

She looked again at Freda, who had exhausted herself quite suddenly and was now embracing a stone carving of a weeping maiden. Hetty leaned over to Cordelia, and said, "I shall call for my man to drive her home."

"That would be for the best."

Both women rose in silent accord, and approached Freda carefully, as if she were a young horse they did not want to startle.

"I ought to be grateful to them," she whispered as she clung to the stone angel, hiding her face. "I suppose that all those women keep him away from *me*, at least."

CHAPTER TWENTY-ONE

After parcelling Freda into the doctor's gig to see her home safely, Cordelia took her leave of Hetty and was driven home herself by Geoffrey. She relaxed into the cushions of the carriage, reflecting on the latest news.

So, the investigation was over, then, was it? No. That could not be allowed. She still knew nothing of the young man's family; but he seemed to be unmourned and unmissed. And she had to find a culprit.

Was the coroner correct? Was the sheriff correct? Had Thomas Bains simply been killed by a passing madman?

Then why had no one been seen in the area? Madmen were usually conspicuous in their madness.

At least Mrs Hurrell was not going to swing for the crime. Cordelia took comfort in that fact. She was utterly convinced that the landlady had not done it. Even if she had suspected that Mrs Hurrell had done it, there was not enough evidence to be perfectly sure. *And only God could make the final judgement,* Cordelia thought. *Certainly not I. Nor any of us mewling mortals. There is something suspicious about Mrs Hurrell, for sure, but I think it is more to do with her dealings in London than anything else.*

Cordelia closed her eyes. She thought back to the morning of the event. *The note.* From whom did this note originate, and what did it say? Where was it now? If it had not been burned or lost, perhaps the sheriff had it, or maybe the bumbling constable discovered the note, and held it as evidence that Mrs Hurrell was, indeed, telling the truth?

Was the note a ruse? If it were from the murderer himself, then that suggested no madman – no, indeed, such a thing was a calculated act to get Thomas Bains on his own.

Thomas had hit his head as he fell. Perhaps the murderer was an unintentional killer. It was conceivable, of course, that the murderer had wanted to speak to Thomas, privately. They might have argued – Thomas being well known for wilful disagreement. The death might have been accidental, and the murderer fled in horror.

It was possible.

Cordelia imagined herself standing once more in the dark cottage room. She pondered the drawer of papers. Mrs Hurrell had her own secrets.

But then, she had to say, did not all women have their private drawers, their hidden letters, their secret lists or notes or diaries? Mrs Hurrell could have reacted because she thought there was something in there – that was not in there. Who could say?

Cordelia knew that her suspicions might be simple flights of fancy, conjured by an underused brain seeking novelty and distraction.

Yes, Ewatt Carter-Hall was a man with secrets, though his secret love affairs were clearly not so well-hidden. And Freda had her own sadnesses though again, they seemed to be worn on her sleeve for all to see. The doctor had a tale or two in his past, but she thought that Carter-Hall's interest in the doctor was more interesting than the doctor himself.

The doctor's wife, the dear Hetty, was so pleasant and agreeable that even that fact could be seen in a suspicious light.

And if she were extending her list of suspects, Cordelia thought, then why not add Ralph Goody to the list? He had argued with Thomas, and–

Her eyes flew open at that. Things seemed to fall into place and she sat forwards, and suddenly noticed that the carriage was stopped, all was quiet, and the door was open. She blinked, and rubbed her eyes, and peered out to find that they were in the stable yard behind Hugo's house.

Geoffrey was sitting on a low wall, picking at his nails with a pocket-knife. He looked up and nodded.

"Was I asleep?" she asked.

"Yes, you were, my lady, and I didn't like to wake you." He came forward to help her down from the carriage.

"Thank you." Still in a daze, she made towards the path that ran to the front of the house so that she might enter by the main doors, but after three steps, she paused, and turned back to Geoffrey.

"Geoffrey. One hour after dinner, will you send Stanley to meet me here?"

He narrowed his eyes, but nodded.

* * *

Dusk was gathering when she slipped out of the house

and around to the stable yard. She was dressed in her finery and had endured a slow and silent dinner with Hugo, who had glowered at her from the far end of the table. She took the chance to creep away when Hugo had taken off to drink some brandy and smoke a cigar with an old friend who had happened by.

It was cool and she pulled her shawl tight around her shoulders. Stanley was already waiting, leaning by the mounting block. He jerked to attention but kept his eyes low.

She wondered if Geoffrey was hiding in the shadows, listening.

"Stanley, thank you. I have a task for you but you must listen carefully. And I need you to act with authority."

"M-m-m?"

She wasn't sure if he were saying "me?" or "my lady" but it hardly mattered. She pulled out a sheaf of letters and hastily written notes from where she had been holding them under her shawl.

"You are to go to Liverpool," she said.

His eyes widened, reflecting the lights from the windows of the back of the house. He didn't even try to speak.

"Yes," she carried on, as if he had questioned her. "I am aware it is some distance hence. I will ask Geoffrey to take you to Cambridge to catch the next train. I have no idea of the changes you will need to make to effect your journey – I tried to make sense of the timetables but I was completely defeated. This is why I say you must act with your own authority. You will be on your own, and making your decisions. I trust you. I have a quantity of money for you to use."

Geoffrey would have been a more confident choice, but she didn't want him returning to her with a trail of bodies behind him. His ways of extracting information were not the ones she really needed at that moment.

She passed Stanley a bag that she had had looped at her waist. In it were a number of bank notes from a London bank, more easily changed than the notes issued by the provincial banks scattered around the country. She had also filled it with coin and some certificates that he might exchange. "Do hide the various things around your person," she counselled him. "If you are robbed or pickpocketed, then you should not lose the whole."

"P-p-p?"

"And if the worst should happen," she continued, "here is an address for you to go to. Indeed, I wish you to seek this person out anyway, as soon as you arrive in Liverpool. I have written to them and they will know to assist you in all ways. I suggest you commit the address to memory."

"B-b-but ... my task, my lady?"

"I want to know everything about Doctor Donald Arnall. I want to understand his past, his dealings, and his first marriage. What became of Clara Arnall? Discover everything, no matter how slight. In particular, has he any enemies? And if you find out that Ewatt Carter-Hall has any connections to him or to Liverpool, then that is of particular importance."

She handed the stunned Stanley the letters. "Here. Some are letters of introduction to people who will answer your questions."

"B-b-but, I cannot." He looked absolutely horrified.

"You are not asking as *yourself*, Stanley," she said, as gently as she could. "You are representing me. You are acting as my proxy. It is not your voice which speaks to these people, but my own, speaking through you. And the letters will open the way for it all. I know many people and I am sure that some of these will assist you. And not all of the letters and notes are addressed to high born folks, either. You will need to speak to prison guards and hospital staff, also. I am sure that you can accomplish this. I would ask no other to do this for me. I trust you."

Of all her staff, he was also the least likely to make off with the considerable sums of money that she had given him.

"How l-long?" he asked.

She hesitated for a moment. "I cannot say. On the one hand, I want you to be as speedy as you can, and return swiftly. But do not neglect your duties. You must be thorough. This, then, is on your own initiative."

His hands were shaking. "No, I cannot…"

"Yes," she said, firmly now. "You can. And you must. Not, then, for me, if I am not incentive enough. Not even for Clarfields, and our own futures. No."

He looked pained.

"No," she continued. "Do it, rather, for the sake of justice."

"Justice?"

"Yes, justice," she repeated vehemently. She gripped Stanley's upper arm forcefully, making him wince with the shock both of the strength of her grip and the unconventional action. "Do this because it is the right thing to do."

She stopped herself from giving him a stirring lecture to appeal to his religious sensibilities, but she could see that his mind was whirring in the right direction now. He met her gaze very briefly before he blushed and looked away. "Yes, my lady," he said.

Geoffrey stepped out of the shadows, as she had predicted he might.

"Take him to the station," she told him, and strode off back into the house.

* * *

She dashed up the stairs, her head and her body alive with potential. It felt good to be directing the action once more. She had a list now of things she wished to learn more about; Ralph, Thomas's family, Mrs Hurrell, and more.

But it also meant staying here with Hugo Hawke so that she might enjoy – or at least, endure – his hospitality for a little longer. He sprang out of his study as she came onto the landing, and his flushed face spoke of not a little drink.

"He's only gone and left me already," he said, referring to the company he had enjoyed earlier. "And I was just getting started. Don't suppose you want to come in and play a hand? Take your mind off this murder business. Let's not act as enemies, Cordelia."

She smiled through gritted teeth. She did not want to offend him too much, in case he cast her out. All he had to stick to was the strict terms of the wager – there was nothing in there to say he had to accommodate her while she investigated. "Of course. Though if I might ring for a cup of tea, that would be perfect."

"I cannot tempt you to a little glass of something?"

"I am afraid not." She was not risking drunkenness again.

He leaned on the doorframe and cocked his head to one side, grinning wolfishly. "But I can tempt you into my room, though…"

Oh, this was tiresome.

"I rather think it is the offer of a game of cards which I find so alluring," she said breezily and stepped past him, letting her skirts swish against his leather boots.

He made a growling noise in his throat and followed her into the room.

He looked serious and intent. She shook her conscience clear. It was all a game, was it not?

And she didn't mean the cards.

"I shall deal," she told him, and took defiant charge.

CHAPTER TWENTY-TWO

Two days later, Freda unexpectedly called on Cordelia. She had been in the library, reading about the different methods of lighting a fire and how the fuel used would impact on what could be cooked. It was fascinating stuff. She had actually gone to the library to think about connections between Ewatt and Mrs Hurrell and the doctor, but she had grown tired and distractible. It was infuriating, waiting for Stanley to return. She had had no word from him. In the meantime, she talked with Ruby, avoided Hugo, and watched Ralph Goody from afar. She still had her suspicions there.

But Freda would be a welcome diversion. Cordelia descended the stairs and met Freda in the hallway. She searched the banker's wife for signs of what might be intoxicating her this particular day.

Freda smiled warmly. Her hands were not twitching, but nor was she yawning or indolent. *Could she be simply unfettered today? Or maybe*, Cordelia thought, *she had aligned her drug and alcohol use into a better balance.*

"Cordelia," she said, continuing with her uninvited liberty of first name terms. "How lovely to find you at home. I wonder, are you free today?"

That was interesting. Cordelia said, "I am. What did you intend?"

Freda clapped her hands like a little girl. "How wonderful! It is such a fine day. And Ewatt is still away again." She gave an affected little pout at that. "So, I thought we might travel into Cambridge."

"By carriage?"

"Mine is outside and the horses are fresh. It is only mid-morning and we should be there by lunchtime. Oh, do say you will come! I long for company."

Cordelia didn't care much for the quality of company, but the potential for gossip was unrivalled, so she quickly agreed, and went back upstairs to change.

* * *

Cordelia learned a little more about how to manage Freda on the long journey to Cambridge. The carriage was better maintained than the Carter-Hall's house, and though they rocked and had to raise their voices to be heard, it was not an unpleasant journey. She began to treat her firmly, with simple instructions and constant re-focussing, as if Freda was an unruly school girl. She seemed to respond to the almost patronising tone with relief.

Freda wanted direction, Cordelia realised. The poor young woman.

Cordelia probed away, digging for information about Thomas Bains, and in particular, what might be known of his family. She had not been able to discover much from the servants at the manor – not much that they were willing to impart, at any rate.

It turned out to be a subject Freda could expand upon.

"He had done jobs at our house," she said. "Didn't he have a loud voice, though?"

"I never met him."

"No, of course not!" Freda covered her mouth in pretend horror. "Oh goodness, yes, you never did. Well. He was a nice young man, I thought, but he didn't do himself any favours, you know?"

"In what way?" It could be tortuous, prodding Freda towards the right information.

"Oh, that I thought he was a pleasant young man, really, and I do think he was a good man, but he sounded like he was not, if you catch my meaning. He talked a lot about things he knew nothing of. I mean, of course, we all do that, but he was so *loud* about it all. Yet I do think he had a golden heart." Freda smiled winningly. "Oh, do you like that phrase? I do. A golden heart. How lovely. A golden heart. I should have liked to have been a poet."

"Indeed." Cordelia smiled through her gritted teeth. It matched with what she'd heard before: he'd talked himself up, but his deeds had been kind. "And what of a sweetheart? Had he set his cap at anyone?"

That was exactly the sort of thing that Freda loved to talk about, be they rich or poor. Other people's lives were as stories to her. "No!" she exclaimed. "None at all that I heard about! Poor man."

"Oh." Cordelia was disappointed. But just because Freda did not know, it did not follow that there was no sweetheart. There would be a lot that happened amongst

270

the people of the town that Freda would not be privy to. Young couples would conceal who they favoured from the gossips for as long as they could.

"I expected that he would marry soon after his father died," Freda continued. "But maybe his arguments put the girls off."

"Maybe so. And what of his mother?"

"I do not rightly know," Freda said. "I heard rumours that she had run off. But then his father was a drinker, so who can blame her? Oh! Look, there." She began to point through the window.

All that Cordelia could see was a loose horse, its reins flapping as it was pursued over a field by a fat man. Then they were past the scene, but Freda was laughing. Such small things delighted the woman, and now she was telling Cordelia all about the pony she had had as a child, and the naughty things that the pony did. Cordelia smiled politely as she listened.

* * *

Cambridge was a vibrant town, replete with tourists

and students and rich and poor alike. They found an elegant hotel which could serve them a very fine midday meal, which they took in a private booth. When it came to pay for the food and service, Freda began to fret and fumble with her purse so Cordelia stepped in to cover the bill. Freda, blushing furiously, began to insist that she pay Cordelia back. It made an unseemly scene and Cordelia hushed her angrily.

For a few minutes Freda sulked silently, until Cordelia realised she had to relent and "make it up to her" even though she did not see that it was her own fault. Falsely bright, she said, "Come, now, Freda. Let us walk and gaze through the shop windows!"

Freda perked up instantly.

But it was soon apparent that it was not enough to simply window-shop. Not for Freda, at least. She darted into shop after shop, and positively plagued the assistants with her demands to see fabrics and furs, hats and ribbons, elegant spoons and ingenious carvings, imported clocks and curious ornaments. There wasn't a mechanical tin soldier in the town that she had not cooed over.

And she bought things, too, but never paid for a

solitary item herself; it was all to be added to Ewatt's accounts, or the bills to be sent on to their house.

It was a dangerous game, Cordelia thought. Freda could accrue no debts of her own, of course, as a married woman; Ewatt would be liable for all of this.

"Might you show a little restraint?" Cordelia said as Freda suddenly grasped her hand and pulled Cordelia towards the open doors of an inn.

"Life is short," Freda shot back airily. "We have but few pleasures in life. Mine is to be a connoisseur of fine things!"

Cordelia thought that Freda didn't really understand what she was saying. There was no chance to remonstrate with her. The inn had large bills tacked up on either side of the doors; a public auction was in progress, and Freda could not wait to enter.

Cordelia followed, with a sinking feeling in her heart.

* * *

That sinking feeling proved to have been entirely justified.

"But I cannot simply take it away this instant!" Freda wailed.

Cordelia took one more step backwards and surveyed the unfortunate scene from a distance. They were standing in the courtyard at the back of the inn, and the auction inside was still progressing. However, the yard was alive with people coming and going. Carts jostled against each other, their axles catching, and the horses baulking. Men in rough brown clothes shouted and cursed as they loaded and unloaded furniture and sundries.

From what Cordelia could make out, a rich businessman on the far side of Cambridge, one Isaac Withington, had gone suddenly bankrupt – well, not he himself, but his businesses had folded, one by one, the collapse of the first sparking a whole chain of slow and inevitable disaster. Now his entire estate was being sold off, and his creditors circled, waiting to seize upon the spoils.

It was said that he had attempted to run for parliamentary office, simply to try and evade being arrested for his debts; no one engaged on political business could be stopped and taken. But that had failed, as he had misunderstood the details of that exclusion, and now he was ruined.

His primary business had been banking, and Freda had gloated in particular about that. "Oh, my Ewatt is such a clever man!" she had repeatedly crowed while in the auction hall, suddenly proud of her husband.

Freda was not showing much pride now they were in the courtyard. In fact, Cordelia could see that the mercurial woman's lightning moods had swiftly become full of fear.

"It will not fit in our carriage! Oh, what am I to do?" She pressed her hands to her throat and her eyes were shining with genuine tears.

The porter was unaffected. He rested his hand on the sideboard. It was of solid teak, and stood five feet high and seven feet wide. "You are to take it, madam, that is what you are to do. For you have bought it."

"I cannot!" She turned to petulance, and stamped her foot. "I shall leave it here."

"That, madam, would be littering, of a most monumental nature."

Cordelia caught the eye of another porter who was standing to one side to watch the show. "Might we engage a carter to deliver it?" she said to him.

"Of course," the man said. "It would be sensible, would it not?"

"Sense, alas, I fear is lacking." Cordelia stepped forward with a heavy sigh, and began to arrange for the sideboard's delivery.

* * *

In spite of Cordelia's direction, Freda then proceeded to cry all the way home. Whatever substances she took to balance her mood were either wearing off, or building up. Cordelia could not tell which. But the result was that Freda sobbed and wailed about what Ewatt was going to say to her when he returned from his trip.

"He ought not to let you out of the house if you cannot be trusted," Cordelia muttered in exasperation, and that triggered a fresh bout of hysterics.

"He usually does not let me out," Freda sniffed. "I have been quite locked up before now! I promised him most faithfully that this time I would behave. Oh, oh, he will be so dreadfully disappointed in me. He hates me to fritter away his hard-earned money."

Cordelia was starting to dislike Ewatt and Freda both. After all, she reflected, he was frittering his money away on his women and his lovers and his trips; the least he could do would be to staff his house better, and treat his wife with more care. She could not quite determine with whom the greater fault rested.

When they rolled up to the front entrance of Hugo's house so that Cordelia could alight, Freda grabbed Cordelia's hands and held them tight. Her eyes were red and her face quite blotchy.

"Do not tell him," she said, imploringly.

Cordelia tried to ease her way to the open door of the carriage. Freda would not let go. Cordelia ended up standing on the gravel, reaching up and over the step awkwardly to where Freda leaned out of the carriage. Geoffrey stood behind Cordelia, muttering under his breath, while waiting to escort her up the steps to the doors.

"I never betray a confidence," Cordelia said. She was not sure what Freda wanted concealing. She was hardly going to be able to hide a sideboard.

"Do not tell him … anything," Freda said, and she gulped in a sob and flung herself back into the carriage, pulling the door closed with a slam.

Cordelia turned, and Geoffrey gave her a long, appraising look before he led her up the stone steps into Hugo's house.

CHAPTER TWENTY-THREE

Cordelia sat in the glass-walled garden room at the back of the house. Rain was pattering incessantly on the roof and against one side. The running water over the glass made the gardens blur into a soft mass of greens with splashes of unidentified colour at intervals. It was a pleasing effect.

Or at least, it had been a pleasing effect for the first hour or so.

Now she was sick of it.

It had been many days since she had sent Stanley north to seek out information about the doctor. She had less than a week left before Hugo went north to join the autumn hunts, and she would lose her house.

When she was in Hugo's company, he was as perfectly attentive as any woman could wish. But the undercurrent of the wager was like a chasm between them. How could he speak with her, flirt with her even, as if nothing had happened? It was as if he thought she'd crumble and accept his offer of marriage.

She would *not*.

He mentioned her sad loneliness, and her uncertain future, and the security of his estates, with regularity.

He did not, at any point, attempt to compromise her, by word or by deed, and that was his one saving grace. She did not feel vulnerable in his presence.

But she had, at last, received a letter from Stanley.

Cordelia held it now in her hands. Ruby was sitting opposite, making a half-hearted attempt to sew the seams flat in the French manner on a new nightdress.

"My lady? May I ask, what does the letter say? I know it is from the daft boy."

"You didn't read it?" Her duplicity was surprisingly lacking. Cordelia assumed she had no secrets from her maid. "Well, then. He confirmed that he had seen, with his own eyes, the marriage register of Clara to the doctor. And then the tales of how she had fled from him!"

"And then what happened to her?"

"I do not know. Perhaps she lives still, and that means

his marriage now is a sham? He is a petty bigamist. Or perhaps he pursued her, and killed her. That's Ewatt's insinuation."

"And you think this means he killed Thomas Bains, also? For what ends?" Ruby said, her brows lowered in concentration.

"The doctor is an awfully good man on the outside," Cordelia said. "But listen. Let us go over this. He had argued with Thomas, and refused to see him. What does that say? There is more. Freda Carter-Hall has a sick child but she does not call the doctor. Why? Perhaps they, too, have argued. Or maybe he has refused to see them, too, but she has covered for him!"

"Were not both Carter-Hall and the doctor at the dinner party that was held here?"

"Yes," Cordelia said. "But they spoke not at all. In fact the doctor kept himself to himself. His wife did not attend. I feel that he was simply making up the numbers."

"We did see him on the day of the murder."

"Indeed we did. And remember, he was riding away, and he was agitated. When he came in, he was wet – oh, the bathing in rivers is an excuse, do you see? He was washing the blood from his body, his hands."

"Oh!"

"You begin to follow my reasoning," Cordelia said. "It seems clear that–"

The door to the hallway opened and Cordelia froze as footsteps clacked over the parquet flooring.

It was Hugo's housekeeper. "My lady; your boy, Stanley, is returned. Shall I send him to you?"

"Where is he?"

"Currently in the kitchens, eating all the bread."

"I shall come down."

"But–"

"Thank you," Cordelia said. She rose and nodded to Ruby, who followed behind.

* * *

The kitchen was full of staff and servants. Stanley sat at the long wooden table, stuffing his face with food. At the other end of the table, two maids were working; one was kneading bread and the other was filling a pie. Another flitted in and out from the scullery with vegetables to be prepared. By the range, Mrs Kendal was stirring a pot, and Mrs Unsworth was at another table by the door to the meat stores, trimming some red carcase of meat that Cordelia could not identify.

Everything stilled as Cordelia appeared at the door. Ruby slipped past her and pulled a chair from the fire to the table, placing it opposite Stanley so that Cordelia could sit down.

Mrs Kendal was as rigid as a poker and she stared, but could not speak.

Cordelia felt the antagonism rolling off the manor house's cook. She smiled sweetly. "Good day, Mrs Kendal. What an industrious kitchen you rule. Mrs Unsworth, some tea when you have a moment."

Mrs Kendal glared, wide-eyed, as Cordelia took the chair and sat herself down. Stanley put his bread down, but she urged him to finish his meal before he spoke to her.

Mrs Kendal said, "The housekeeper's room might ... perhaps my lady would be more comfortable ... I can arrange..."

"No, thank you. I wish to speak to Stanley and he is busy here."

One by one, the various servants melted away in embarrassment until only Cordelia, Stanley, Ruby and Mrs Unsworth were left. Even Mrs Kendal had found important business elsewhere to attend to.

Stanley still stammered as he spoke, and kept his eyes lowered. But he talked with more ease than he had done previously. "My lady. It is true that Clara, the doctor's first wife, fled from him," he said.

"Ill-treatment?" she asked.

"By whom? Not him, by all accounts. Everyone said that he treated her kindly. No, she was a woman who did not ... I mean she ... her allotted place did not suit ... she ran away, in short."

"Oh. She was a flighty sort, was she?"

Stanley blushed. "Indeed, my lady, she was an unsuitable match. She went away with a travelling merchant."

"And then?"

"This was six years ago. There was no word of her that could be got. And the doctor himself sought for her, but to no avail. Then the doctor married his present wife, two years ago."

"But he was already married!"

"Indeed. If he had waited then he could have done so without disgrace."

"Seven years," Cordelia mused. After that period of time, a missing person could be assumed dead. "But he waited only ... let me see. Four years. Oh dear; the foolish man. And what of this Clara now?"

"She is dead, and I have seen her death certificate."

"All is well, then! Obviously not for Clara," Cordelia added hastily. "But for the doctor…"

"Maybe. For she died but one year ago."

"So, our good doctor *was* a bigamist," Cordelia said. "Although now she is dead, does it still count? I am hazy on the legal details."

Ruby interrupted. "But did he know that he was committing a crime? That would seem to be an important point."

"I think he must have done. It is only recently that he has begun to ask after the whereabouts of his first wife. If he had no evidence that she was dead – for when he married again, she was not dead – then he ought not to have married. He knew he was wrong."

"I wonder if his current wife knows this tale?" Ruby

said.

"If she does not, then it ought to stay that way," Cordelia advised. "Now that Clara is dead, it would profit no one for this sad truth to be revealed."

Stanley sat back in his chair, and swept up the crumbs into his hand to brush them onto the platter before him. "I learned a lot about the man," he said slowly, containing his words carefully. "And though he might have been a bigamist, not one person that knew him could countenance his being a murderer. No one but God knows the secret substance of a man's heart, but … but … it seems unlikely that Donald Arnall was the man who killed Thomas Bains."

"I agree," said Cordelia, and a feeling of heavy glumness washed over her. "Now I think on it, the whole edifice of my assumptions and suspicions seem silly and vague. Now where do I look?"

Mrs Unsworth shook her head with a suppressed laugh. "You will perhaps look back to the very beginning." Everyone turned to look at her. For the sagging older woman to volunteer any information beyond complaints or bile was so unusual that everyone wanted to listen to her. She basked in her moment of glory and attention.

"What is it?" Cordelia urged.

"Mrs Hurrell has fled to London, the very moment that she was released."

Cordelia sat in stunned silence as she digested it. Ruby made to speak but she was silenced instantly by a wave of Cordelia's hand.

Eventually, she said, "She has fled? Does that, then, prove her guilt after all?"

Again, Ruby opened her mouth but Cordelia went on, overriding her. "And if the murderer – the murderess! – was Mrs Hurrell all along, playing a convincing game, then it was my meddling that turned the coroner and the sheriff against the idea. It was my suggestion that had the constable look elsewhere for his clues. Me! And my meddling that has deflected all the investigation from the true solution, and now the killer, once under lock and key, walks free again! Fled, fled to London. Oh, no. The newspaper. The note must have been fake. There is something else, something I am missing…"

"But my lady," Ruby broke in at last. "She was held and she was subjected to scrutiny. She was originally from London, was she not? She is a poor woman and alone.

Would you not flee, in her situation, the moment that you could? Does it prove her guilt, or just prove her *defencelessness?*"

Cordelia toyed with the cooling cup of tea in front of her, and could not answer.

Chapter Twenty-Four

Gradually, the servants floated back into the kitchen. Cordelia ignored their sideways glances for as long as she could, but eventually she stood up and nodded at Stanley.

"Thank you for your service," she said. "You have done remarkably well, and I am very grateful. It has stopped raining, I believe. Will you escort me into town?"

He lurched to his feet, his elbows jutting out as fought his gangly body to a stiff pose of attention. "My lady."

Ruby was on her feet then, too. "And I?"

"No; my dresses need looking over. And I want to talk to Stanley further."

"But–"

"You may fetch my gloves and bonnet, of course, Ruby. I shall meet you in the hallway. Come, Stanley."

"But–"

Cordelia ignored Ruby's sudden petulance, and sallied out of the kitchen, closely followed by Stanley. She heard Ruby say something indelicate, and Mrs Unsworth said something back but Ruby then pushed past them both at the doorway and ran the opposite way along the corridor to go up the servants' stairs to Cordelia's rooms.

Mrs Unsworth appeared and started to say, "You come back here and…" but she stopped as Cordelia half-turned. Mrs Unsworth's face was purple but she retreated back into the kitchen.

Soon, Cordelia was striding out, pattens on her feet to keep her skirts clear of the mud. There were puddles all along the road, the rain unable to soak away quickly because the ground was so dry from long days of hot sun. It was pleasantly refreshing to be in the sparkling post-storm air, even if it did mean a deal more work for Ruby upon Cordelia's return.

Stanley walked a half-pace behind, and did not presume to initiate any conversation.

She had no destination in mind. She simply wanted to walk. After a short while of mulling things over, she said, "Stanley, what do you think about the murder of Thomas

Bains?"

"I don't know, my lady."

"You do. You think on these things."

"I think about my immortal soul, mostly," he said morosely.

"Please, speak freely. You do not think that the doctor is responsible?"

"I do not, my lady. He has sinned, it is true. But not as a killer. Still, it is not for me to judge."

"But judge we must, here on this earth," she insisted. "It is a matter of justice, as I said to you before."

"And that justice is for better people than I to pursue," he said.

"Are we not all equal before God?" she said. She hoped she didn't sound as if she were mocking his fervent beliefs.

"We are, but we all have our allotted stations in life. Some are given to lead and others to follow, my lady. We may be equal in our souls but certainly we cannot be all the same in our duties or our positions. If all are kings, who then serves?"

Who indeed. "But Geoffrey is encouraging you to think higher," she said.

"He does but he thinks only of material things."

"Are you never tempted?"

He paused before he stammered out, "Always, my lady. By many things both mundane and terrifying. But I pray on the Lord and I will be saved, if He wills it so. He lends me strength in hard times."

"That strength had to be within you anyway," she said.

"No, my lady. I achieve nothing with Him."

"Hmm." All her years of Bible study and regular Church attendance had made little impression on her; the long debates that appeared in the press held no interest for her. She was interested, however, in how faith made Stanley act and think. She said, on an impulse, "What do you think about Hugo Hawke?"

"I respect him as a gentleman," Stanley said stiffly.

"And as a human?"

"He is a gentleman," he repeated, and she wondered if he thought those things were mutually exclusive.

"Should I marry him?" she asked. "Accept my fate and be done with it all?"

He was silent and she thought she might have pushed him too far. But when she glanced at him, she saw he was deep in contemplation.

"It is not good for you to be on your own," he said at last. "Though if you were to throw yourself into good and charitable works, as many widows do, then that would be the best option of them all."

"I ought to be a philanthropist rather than marry?" she asked.

"You ought to be a philanthropist rather than marry Mr Hawke," he said, correcting her and stammering dreadfully. He began to apologise but she cut him off.

"No, I understand. Thank you."

"But if it comes down to temptation, and if that is becoming too strong, then you must marry," he said in a rush.

They walked on. *Temptation*, she thought. That word again. "Temptation comes in many forms."

"Money, most of all," Stanley said.

"Indeed it does." *Oh yes. Money.*

They came to the outskirts of the town. She stopped and said, "I think we will turn back here. Thank you for your company."

He muttered a reply and they began to wander back to

the manor house. Her pace slowed. She felt heavy, as if she did not want to return.

"Stanley, do you know anything of Mrs Hurrell?"

"Nothing, my lady. Save that she was the landlady where Thomas Bains was killed."

"She holds a mystery too."

"But she is gone, as they did say."

"Back to where she came from," Cordelia said. She gave a groan of frustration. "Oh! I should have sent you to London to ask about her, not had you running to Liverpool to dig up dirt on a man who is guilty of mistakes but not of murder. I have erred and time is short. I may have lost Clarfields on this wild goose chase."

"I can travel to London if you wish."

It was tempting but she sighed deeply. "Do you think there is any point?"

"It is not for me to say, my lady."

Oh, the frustrating and pious little ... she shook her head. No, Stanley was as Stanley was. *What tempted him*, she wondered as they completed the journey in silence.

And what was her own temptation?

CHAPTER TWENTY-FIVE

Maybe it was time to accept it was a woman's lot in life to be forever in the dark, on the outside, not quite part of society; society was made by men, for men. The coroner and the sheriff had made up their minds about the murder. And so life moved on.

Too quickly.

It irked Cordelia beyond measure. There was no time to waste now. She took a hurried luncheon, and went straight back out again. She was not going to lurk around in conservatories, spending endless hours on pretty embroideries while she waited for some man that she didn't even love to propose marriage to her. How ridiculous was that! And as for Hugo and his stupid wager … She shook herself free of it all, armed herself with her breeding and her determination, and resolved to ignore the feeling of constriction and doom that even now seemed to follow her as she strode along the gravel path that led away from Hugo's manor.

She wondered how Freda was getting on, and whether Ewatt had returned home and discovered the sideboard and the pile of bills. She let her feet carry her in the direction of their house, and instead of sinking into pointless introspection, she paid a closer attention to what she saw.

She was beginning to see that the Carter-Halls were not as rich as they might like others to believe they were. Of course, so many people presented a false view to the world. The little she understood of business led her to understand that much money did not even exist in reality. Some companies were built entirely on a promise or an idea or possible future profits. And she could readily accept that Ewatt's business interests waxed and waned, from periods of plenty to occasional famine. The newspaper article had shown her that. She felt sure she'd missed something there, but it was the news about Ewatt that stuck in her mind. *The silly man ought to let his wife into his confidence,* she thought crossly; *so much trouble might be saved that way. If only people would speak plainly!*

She came to the wide gates that stood open, and stopped to look around her. The gates, indeed, were rusted at the hinges; never could they close. She let her eye wander down the sweeping driveway. Now she could see weeds at the edges of the path, and the grass lawn made a ragged line against the gravel. Ralph Goody would not allow such laxity.

She studied the house. From this distance, it looked like any other. As she approached, however, she noted now the peeling paintwork on the window frames, and the scuffs on the stone steps. She had seen this before but now she looked with fresh understanding.

The only thing of any cleanliness was a wooden post box which was affixed to the wall to the side of the door, and half-hidden by a round stone column that supported a balcony above the front door. It was freshly painted in blue. She was looking at it when she was surprised by the door opening, and Ewatt appeared.

He seemed as startled to see her as she was to see him. "Did you ring?" he said, and then quickly followed that with, "I am sorry! How rude of me. I mean to say, good day to you, my lady Cornbrook ... and also, did you ring?"

"I did not. I was about to," she said hastily.

"Ah; good. I thought for a minute that one more thing had gone awry!"

"I am curious as to your post box," she said. "When the penny post came in, I sent for the carpenters directly and they cut a fresh smart hole in my door. Hugo has done the same at the manor. But you have created this; is it not easier to have your letters simply appear in your hallway?"

He harrumphed, and then laughed. "What, let some wood-butcher hack a hole in my fine oak door? Nonsense, dear woman. Allow me some standards."

As if I have none. And that door is not oak; you must think my head is oak if you assume I will believe that. She smiled. "Of course."

A shadow crossed Ewatt's face and he stopped smiling as he looked at the box. "I am sad to say, though, that it is a poignant reminder of that poor lad who died. It was Thomas who came to fit it for me."

"Indeed? And have you heard; no one is to be tried for the murder."

"I heard. It does not seem right, in truth, but I suppose they know the facts. Anyway!" He jerked his head up and forced a smile back onto his face. "Enough of this maudlin talk. What of you? Is this a social call? Are you staying longer with old Hugo? Has he made an honest woman of you yet?"

She wondered if he knew of the wager that had been drawn up after his drunken departure. She decided she didn't want to become the topic of new gossip yet so she smiled as enigmatically as she could.

"I am on a social call. I wondered if your Freda was at home. I know you said, before, that I ought to check before…"

His smile, unconvincing from the first, was dashed away once more. She began to understand the cause of his sadness as he explained. "She is unavailable, I am afraid. And I fear that she will be unavailable for some time."

"Is she ill?"

"In a manner of speaking, yes."

"Have you sent for the doctor?" Cordelia asked, and it was deliberately done to see Ewatt's reaction. *He would not call him for the children, but surely for his wife…*

And Ewatt shook his head, his brows lowering. "Sadly, my wife's … lack of care in her … interests … are part of the problem and the doctor, esteemed though he might be in medical matters, is not entirely welcome here. Some men of power let it go to their heads, perhaps. It is always a dangerous thing, do you not think, when a man is alone with a woman, especially a delicate woman such as my dear Freda? Male doctors and female patients … emotions run so high … no good can come of it."

Goodness. What was he suggesting? That Freda had been conducting an affair with Donald Arnall? Cordelia tipped her head to one side. For the wife to behave that way – oh, it was a very different thing indeed to Ewatt's dalliances. The woman must remain pure. "I am so very sorry to hear that," Cordelia said sympathetically, even as she thought, *but why must it be such a different thing?*

Ewatt sighed. "There is hope. There is always hope. Today, I sent for an eminent doctor from Cambridge, who comes highly recommended. He specialises in feminine disorders of the mind, hysteria, wayward wombs, that sort of thing. I am dreadfully afraid that I …"

"What is it?" Cordelia reached out a hand to his trembling shoulder.

"I must face the awful fact that she might be *completely* … unwell. She needs … proper care. Away from here. Do you understand?"

Cordelia understood perfectly and her heart ached for them both. His usually florid speech was staccato with pain. He meant that she might need to be committed into an asylum. "It could be a temporary respite of great success," she said. "A few weeks of proper care, as you say, and she could return as a new woman. Trust in the medical man, and trust to science and new methods of treating such things."

He nodded. "You are right. Thank you. You have been a good friend to me," he said sincerely.

"If there is anything more I might do—"

"I shall not hesitate. Thank you."

She bid him good day and turned. As she walked away, she pondered on the turn of events. It was true, what Ruby had said; she was getting to know the people here, and she liked them. Even Freda, with her irritating habits, was at times a likeable woman. Ewatt was in debt, that much was now obvious. He was hiding it, and that made him untrustworthy even if he was easily understood.

And the doctor?

Cordelia asked herself if she really thought that the

doctor might be having an affair with Freda. She could believe it of Freda. But of Donald Arnall?

Actually, she thought – perhaps. *He is exceedingly modern in his lifestyle,* she reminded herself. All that brown bread and the unhealthy fondness for vegetables. Was he also modern in his morality? Did he follow those that railed against the time-honoured institutions of marriage, and clamoured for a "new way" of living? Such cranks were known, but usually ignored.

Had she ignored something very important about the doctor, she asked herself.

And if so, what was she going to do about it?

CHAPTER TWENTY-SIX

That afternoon, she walked with a purpose into the high-ceilinged kitchen, and straight into the middle of an argument.

Mrs Unsworth had a ladle in her hand and she was brandishing it aloft. Her face was red and pearled with sweat, and she was breathing heavily, gripping the back of a chair with her other hand.

On the other side of the table, hands on her hips and her head tipped defiantly back, stood Ruby. She, too, was flushed. "I wouldn't want to take anything you'd touched anyway, you old–"

Both fell silent instantly as Cordelia clapped her hands. It wasn't a loud noise, but it drew their attention. It was her presence which silenced them.

In a carefully low voice, she said, "What is going on?

Mrs Unsworth. You speak first."

Ruby bridled at that, and Cordelia heard her tut.

Mrs Unsworth snarled towards Ruby, but lowered the
ladle. "My lady," she mumbled. "This skilamalink hussy is
nothing but a low gutter-bred thief!"

"I am *not*," shrieked Ruby but Cordelia threw out a
pointed finger, and commanded her to hush.

Mrs Unsworth flared her nostrils like a bull before
continuing. "It is common knowledge that food has been
going missing here," she said. "And I tell you that it is *she*."

Ruby flung her hands in the air, and said, simply, "Your
proof?"

"Indeed," Cordelia said. "Do you have evidence for
this claim, Mrs Unsworth?"

"Missing food!" Mrs Unsworth declared. "Constantly.
Ask any of the staff here."

"It is true that I had heard of missing food," Cordelia
said. "Did not Ralph Goody suggest it was Thomas Bains?
And in any case, when I ask for evidence, I mean, what
evidence have you that it was Ruby?"

Mrs Unsworth huffed. "Well," she muttered, "just look
at her."

"That's all your proof?"

This time, Mrs Unsworth was silent.

Cordelia could feel the tension in the air. It had been brewing for a long time. It was unfair to ask her own cook to share another cook's kitchen and it was uncomfortable for her staff to try and settle in here.

She thought about the figure she had seen, a week or so ago, that night; it had been carrying a bundle. *It?* On reflection, she felt sure it was male, with a man's broad shoulders and peaked cap.

There were things that were tied together, here, she thought. *Nothing is separate. It's all linked. And* she began to think she might know who was stealing food, and who was the murderer too.

But she had no evidence and she could see no way of getting it. Like the scene before her, it could not be resolved. It was evidence she needed, more than anything else. She snapped her fingers. "Ruby, go up to my rooms. Mrs Unsworth, take the afternoon off."

Ruby and Mrs Unsworth glared at one another. But they ducked to obey.

CHAPTER TWENTY-SEVEN

Cordelia walked sluggishly back to her suite of rooms, and found Ruby standing by the window. She was staring out over the green lawns, her hand resting on the wooden frame. She glanced over her shoulder as Cordelia entered.

"Ruby. Tell me about the troubles you're having with Mrs Unsworth."

Ruby turned back to the glass once more, her chin tilted. She spoke to the view. "I am not the one having troubles; it is she."

"You are very different people."

"No," Ruby said. "I think we are the same person at different times in one life. Don't you think?"

"What do you know of Mrs Unsworth and her past?" Cordelia asked curiously.

"What anyone can tell from looking at her; a sad

widow, or maybe abandoned. Dead family. No friends. She never says."

Cordelia had been holding her breath. She let it go slowly. *Ruby didn't know.* "You are right in parts," she said. "And tell me another thing. The truth, mind. Are you stealing food?"

Ruby turned and leaned against the window frame, nestling her shoulder into the heavy crimson drapes. "No more than any servant ever does, my lady," she said. "After all, all the fine stuff is under lock and key. The butler and the housekeeper see to all that. I could never pilfer tea or brandy or sugar or spices. But yes, of course, I may take a heel of bread or a rind of cheese from time to time. Why should the pigs or the midden have the waste? However, as to Mrs Unsworth's accusations, no. I do not steal what she says I do. But it makes one wonder, do you not think?"

"It makes me wonder who is taking it."

"No," Ruby said, shaking her head lightly, and she smiled slightly. "They have taken large items. A wheel of cheese, a side of meat. So, for one, they are strong. And secondly, the amount that has gone, over time, I would wager that they are selling it. This is not the act of a hungry servant, my lady."

"You are right," said Cordelia. "It is a business, indeed, and nothing to do with Thomas Bains. Perhaps."

"So, what do you do now, my lady?" Ruby asked boldly. "What have you lately discovered?"

"I offended you when I chose Stanley to walk me into town, did I not?" Cordelia said.

"Not at all," Ruby replied, the offence writ plain upon her face. "I am just your maid."

They both knew it was not true. Cordelia laughed. "Come now. The passing weeks have been so strange that I think everything has changed, at least in my own household, and you a part of it. Anyway, I needed Stanley's clear vision, and a different opinion."

"He has too much of that," Ruby said.

"What do you mean?"

"His clear vision. He *looks* at me, in a way that a man so church-like ought not to," she said. "And I am used to it from most men, because indeed I will it so. I'd be offended if most men did not look. But not from *him*. He is barely a man."

"Oh, Ruby. He admires you."

"No, he thinks I am sinful and wants to save me," she said, sneering. "But he is also ... curious about me. Though, standing twenty feet away and staring at my ankles is the closest he's ever going to get to a woman."

Cordelia felt sorry for Stanley, all tied up in knots. "Well, you must ignore him."

"I do. But still, what did his clear vision tell you?"

Cordelia sighed and sat down on a chair. "That it is better to marry than to be tempted, for one."

Ruby smiled. "He knows nothing. Now, my lady, the murder... time is pressing."

"Don't I know it! Oh, Ruby, I feel as if the more I discover, the more unlikely it is that I shall ever solve it. We lack proof."

Ruby folded her arms. "Everything is proof. When you went into the cottage, and looked and listened, you found proof. When you found me sitting on the wooden chest that had been moved, that was proof. Everything is proof ... now you must knit all of this together."

"You are right."

"There, then. Continue," said Ruby. "We need you."

"Thank you, Ruby." Cordelia closed her eyes in

thought for a moment, standing still in the room, swaying in her self-imposed darkness. When she opened them again, Ruby had not moved.

"I will have an early night," Cordelia declared.

CHAPTER TWENTY-EIGHT

The claim of wanting an early night was, of course, a ruse. Cordelia sent Ruby to Hugo with the message that she was unwell and would not be attending dinner. She could not face the thought of him.

When Ruby returned, Cordelia dismissed her for the evening. "I wish to get into bed, and read my books. Will you simply bring up a tray of food; after that you can please yourself."

Ruby looked at her curiously. "What are you planning, my lady?"

"I need to look at the evidence," she said. "As you told me."

"Hmm." Ruby was obviously not convinced, but she followed orders. When she returned with a tray of cold meats, a salad, pickles and pies, Cordelia was wearing a dressing robe and sitting at her table.

As soon as Ruby had disappeared for the evening, no doubt to an assignation with a footman, Cordelia leaped to her feet and shed the dressing robe to reveal she was dressed very curiously indeed. She was wearing a thin skirt, without layers of petticoats below; indeed, she was feeling rather light and exposed without the cascade of fabric so usual around her legs. Instead she was wearing a particularly long chemise which was nearly as long as the dark skirt. On top of her corset, she wore a tight-waisted riding jacket, and a mantlet. She bound a dark cloth about her hair, and wrapped a scarf around her neck, which she immediately unwound again as she became too hot. She wanted to be able to blend into the shadows, and it was imperative that she was able to move freely, and potentially swiftly.

She prowled around her chambers, snacking on the food from time to time. She passed from window to door to window, as the night gathered and the sounds of the house grew lower and fainter. There was a bottle of wine on the tray as well, and she sipped at a glass for courage.

Finally, she judged it to be time. She picked up the scarf once more, and twisted it around her neck and jaw. With her heart thudding almost painfully, she crept to the door and peered out along the corridor.

There was a lamp still lit at the far end, at the top of the main flight of stairs. All was quiet. She slipped out, walking on the carpet in the centre of the floor so that her boots did not clack on the wooden boards. She paused every few steps, to listen and to look around.

Nothing. No one.

She made it to the hallway but this was a tiled floor. She walked as if on a frozen lake, lowering each foot to the floor in slow motion, endeavouring to move silently. At the main front door, she stopped again. Did it squeak? She could not remember.

No, she said to herself. Ewatt Carter-Hall's door squeaked with lack of maintenance but Hugo was a man intent on good appearances. His door would open perfectly. She took a deep breath, and tried it.

It was silent.

Then she was out on the steps under the pale light of a half-moon that peeped out from scudding grey clouds. Her eyes were by now well-adjusted to the gloom. It was cold, far more cold than she had expected for the summertime. Was that the hint of impending autumn in the air? She took a jump from the bottom step so that she could land on the grass and avoid the crunching gravel. She ran lightly over the lawn to the hedge that bordered it, and used its shadow to hide her as she made for the gates and the track beyond.

She discovered, to her surprise, that she was grinning. After all, the whole enterprise was utterly absurd. She imagined how it might be reported in the London press; *titled widow running amok in country estate*, she thought. From there, they would take her straight to the asylum, just like poor Freda Carter-Hall.

Poor Freda, she thought again, the words becoming like a refrain in her head as she crept through the dark lanes to the house of the Carter-Halls. She stopped by the bottom of their driveway, and studied it, but there was not a single light in any of the windows. Nothing stirred. It was curiously quiet. Too quiet. Was he away again, abroad this time? She hoped so.

She was no longer cold. In fact, she was hot, and unpleasantly sweaty.

No matter, she told herself. *Onwards*. She began to make

a careful progress towards the front door of the house.

But it was not the front door that was her final objective; indeed, she sought the post box to one side of the door. From her belt she drew out a flattened metal tool, about fourteen inches long, that she had tucked there after stealing it from the meat stores. She examined the box carefully before pressing the sharp end of the tool into the hinged side of the door. She pressed it into the slot between the post box's door and the box itself, and then began to lever it to the side.

Nothing budged.

She shifted her grip and leaned, laying her whole weight against it, hoping to burst the door open. The wood began to groan and splinter. She pressed harder, nervousness making her throat dry. She was braced for it to give up, any moment, in a shower of wood shards and noise.

A light went on in the window to the other side of the main door. She froze.

Something clattered from within.

Was it a dropped key?

She pulled at the tool but now it was stuck fast in the post box. The door handle shook and she could hear the sound of a bolt being drawn back, or maybe – if she was lucky – it was only the sound of someone shooting the bolt home.

With a great jerk, she tried to wrestle the tool free, but hesitated by the box, staring at the door. Surely it was someone – that slovenly housekeeper maybe – simply locking up for the night.

Then two arms grabbed her from behind and she was hauled backwards so quickly that she could not even shout. She fought back and they tumbled together into the bushes that ran out at an angle from the corner of the house. She was on her knees, and grabbed instinctively at the assailant's legs so that he fell down too.

As he did so, he put a hand up to her mouth, and pressed hard, and whispered, "My lady, stay down and stay quiet! It is I, S-Stanley."

Cordelia was stunned enough to be unable to move. He removed his hand. She remained frozen, her knees in the cold earth, as Stanley came to her side and knelt as well. They both looked towards the front door.

It opened. The housekeeper peered out, looking down the driveway. Cordelia held her breath. The housekeeper stepped onto the front step and held a lamp aloft. It threw great shadows behind and around her, and it brought particular attention to the tool which stuck out of the post box, creating a monstrous black shape on the wall.

But the housekeeper did not look that way. She was staring down the driveway, frowning. Eventually she stepped back, lowering the lamp as she did so. When she did turn her head left and right, the lamp's angle meant that the post box was not silhouetted, and nothing seemed amiss.

The door closed and the bolts were shot home.

Still they did not move or speak until the lights in the windows were extinguished, and even then Cordelia counted to one hundred before hissing in Stanley's ear the most important question of the night: "What are you doing here?"

He shook his head, a movement she only half-caught. "My lady, l-let's go."

"The file—"

He glanced up at her, his eyes shining white. Without another word, he darted to the box and grabbed the file, wrenching it free, and bounded back to her.

I probably loosened it for him, she thought, amazed at his sudden strength. *The boy has become a man, indeed.*

"Now, we must go!" he urged.

She was so shocked she could not think straight. Like two prowling cats, they made their way stealthily back onto the road, and did not talk until they were halfway back to Hugo's. She could contain herself no longer.

"Stanley, speak! What brought you there?"

"Forgive me, my lady. Geoffrey sent me to watch you."

"Why? Does that infuriating man spy upon me every night?"

Stanley was shocked at the insinuation. "Ab-bsolutely not, my lady. Not every night, there is no need. But he said that you took a file from the meat store, and he was concerned."

"Oh. So he saw that. Well, then. I suppose I ought to thank you for pulling me out of the way."

"My lady, the box is now damaged," Stanley said suddenly. "They will suspect foul play."

"They will. There is nothing to be done about that. And maybe it will flush some game from the undergrowth."

"I see."

He did not. They walked more boldly, keeping to the

centre of the road now. The clouds had dissipated and the way was clear. Eventually, Stanley spoke unbidden, in a rare show of confidence.

"My lady, if I may ask …"

"You wish to know what I did there."

"I do. Forgive my impertinence-"

"There is nothing to forgive, Stanley. You have just rescued me, and so you need make no apology. I was breaking into Ewatt's post box."

"Yes."

She smiled. She could feel his curiosity warring with his servile restraint. After a tortuous moment, she relented, and offered him a greater explanation. "Mr Carter-Hall is a man of secrets and affairs," she said. "That is why he had that post box made. He claimed to be keeping his front door pristine, but that is a blatant lie. No, he did not wish anyone else to see his letters coming."

"That is not so unusual," Stanley said. "The affairs, I mean. He is a man of business, and business is a hotbed of sin and temptation."

"You are quite correct, but not in the way you think you mean," she said. "I wanted to see if I could find correspondence, or hidden things, in there. It was a dangerous trick, I know, and probably doomed to failure."

"Almost certainly," he said. "Why would you chance it? Does he not empty his post box daily?"

"Likely he does. Still, there was another reason. And you will see why I am not worried about the damage we left. For it is a sign, you see."

"For him? But why?"

"He is mixed up in much, and Stanley, I ought to have sent you to London, you know. For Mrs Hurrell is a guilty party in this, and she has thrown me sideways, and yet it is her presence and her deeds that have drawn me back to the motive and the deed itself."

"You cannot think that she did it!"

"In London, she ran a 'respectable' disorderly house. Do you have an idea of what that might mean?"

"Sin," said Stanley firmly.

"And, as you say, business and businessmen are a hotbed of such sin. Indeed. The woman is connected. Connected enough to set up in this town, as a landlady. And no allegations attach to her here, I might add. I believe her current house and business to be a clean one."

"But why would she kill?"

"I do not say that she did. But she knows something, although I rather think she does not know the value of what she knows. And think: why would *anyone* kill? You spoke to me of temptation, of money and of power and of love. What tempted Thomas Bains? I rather think that the hot-headed and loud young man was the most moral and least tempted of us all, Stanley. Who made the post box? It was Thomas Bains."

"Do you think the murderer was a group – a gang of people working together?"

"No, Stanley. But I do think they are all linked, every one of them. The doctor, Ewatt, Freda and Mrs Hurrell. And one of them did it, I am sure of it. No, not a passing vagrant – no. One of those."

"And you seek proof?"

"Proof, somehow," she said. "And maybe I might get that by borrowing some hunting techniques from Hugo. We shall flush the quarry from its den, Stanley."

CHAPTER TWENTY-NINE

Stanley remained silent as he accompanied her back to the house and round to the kitchens. She slipped in and thanked him, and went as quietly as she could back up to her rooms.

Ruby was asleep, or at least, making a passable imitation of it in her room. Cordelia quickly undressed and slid into bed.

She did not sleep for some time.

* * *

"And what will you wear for tonight's party?" Ruby asked the next morning as she attended to Cordelia's hair.

"What party?"

"The one that Hugo arranged ages ago," Ruby said. She dipped her fingers in some styling cream and pulled out some strands, curling them to hang artfully around Cordelia's face. "It still goes ahead, in spite of the recent changes in circumstance. It is the end of summer event."

"Oh, I knew he was to have some small cards game this evening."

"Small cards game? Oh no, my lady. It is a ball, and quite the thing. It was arranged for another reason, my lady, so his servants say. I am afraid that he planned it from the moment you arrived ... it was to be the announcement of your engagement."

"The cad! The beast!" Cordelia exclaimed in dismay. "Why did he not cancel?"

Ruby's hands stilled and came to rest on Cordelia's shoulders. "My lady, he is all about appearance. And front. And face. And ... spite."

"Spite?"

"Yes. For I am sure he means to trap you or humiliate you or something."

"Then why are you asking me what I intend to wear?" Cordelia said. "I shall not go. This would be madness."

Ruby took up a length of ribbon and curled it. "My lady, of course you will go. You would not let him win, would you? We must ensure your dress is of the very best. You need all your armour possible."

Cordelia sighed as deeply as she could, letting her shoulders relax and the tension dissipate. "You are correct, and thank you. Well, so it is to be an extravaganza tonight, is it?"

"It is. All shall be there."

"Interesting. Everyone? I think I shall remain in my rooms today, with a headache."

"I am sorry to hear that, my lady. Shall I send for anything? A cold compress, lavender, Kendal Black Drop—"

Cordelia smiled. "No, my dear. I have a headache in the same way that you go for bracing evening strolls for the sake of your constitution."

"Ah. I see." Ruby smiled and Cordelia caught her eyes in the looking-glass.

"Just bring some food to sustain me," Cordelia said. "I have reading to do, and more importantly; thinking."

* * *

She wore red, that night.

"I need it for confidence," she explained.

"I do not think that you have ever lacked for confidence," Ruby said. "But I agree."

Cordelia smoothed down the satin skirts and adjusted her gloves. "The woman you see before you now is not the girl I once was," she said. "And sometimes that young girl comes back to me. I need to stay here a little longer; I have written most urgently to London for some final information, which will confirm – or perhaps deny – my suspicions. Until then, I must keep on Hugo's good side, such as it is. Or at least, play along."

"Do not let him get the better of you."

"I shall be the better person," Cordelia said airily. She liked the moral sound of it, but how she'd put that into practise, she did not know.

"Stanley would be proud of you," Ruby muttered drily.

"Do you think?" Cordelia smiled as she went to the door. "I doubt it. Now; to battle!"

* * *

Cordelia stopped at the top of the stairs and had to

328

take some calming breaths. She had never before been so scared at a gathering like this; not even in her first marriage, and that had held its own share of particular fear.

She rested her gloved hand on the polished dark wood of the bannister, and studied the crowds, pleading with her logical, rational brain to take over and squash the roiling emotions of her fast-beating heart. It was, perhaps, a stroke of luck that this was just some provincial backwater. There were not quite as many people as there could have been.

But that also meant there were fewer places to hide.

There was the doctor, of course, and his wife. Ewatt was milling about, but there was no sign of Freda. There was a smattering of matrons and girls and young bucks and red-faced men, and one or two military types. Some were familiar from Hugo's earlier dinners and gatherings. Some had such unremarkable faces that she didn't think she would recognise them if she saw them every day.

He must have invited a few of the great and the good from Cambridge. She watched as a couple entered the hallway and were greeted by Hugo's butler. The man shook a shower of drops from his long, dark coat and the woman was sheltering under an upraised cape. When the door opened again she peered and could see the rain outside was of torrential scale. The sleeting rain reflected the lights of the house in diagonal lines, and puddles were forming by the door as people were met by the staff and led away to disrobe.

The tracks and roads would swiftly become mud, she thought. *Still, most will be pleasantly drunk by the time it comes to travel home.* Only their servants, presently supping in the servants' hall, would have to deal with problems they'd encounter on their slog through the morass in the storm.

Ruby appeared at her elbow and looked down at the throng. "Are you well, my lady?" she asked.

"No," Cordelia confessed. "For, looking at this now, I do not see how I might avoid Hugo. There are not enough people for me to hide from him in the crowd. Oh, perhaps I have miscalculated, Ruby."

"Well, let us be sensible," Ruby said, sounding older than she was. It made Cordelia almost smile. "If this has, indeed, been a misjudgement. You can do one of a few things. You can retreat back to your rooms and pretend dire illness. That would be easy enough. I can even poison you a little, if you like."

"Sounds … less than tempting, but thank you for the offer."

"You're welcome. Well, then. You can run away. I've done it plenty of times. It is probably a little harder for you, but we can all gather up your things."

Cordelia looked down the sweeping stairs and imagined running down them and bursting through the front doors. It had a certain tempting drama about it. "No, I think not," she said reluctantly. "I have a few days left and I must *try*, at least. I must stay to the bitter end of all this."

"You can, then, brazen it out, my lady. Play him along. Play a game of your own. You are a woman, and we can all do these things."

It was true. Cordelia knew female friends who had not told a single truth in well over a decade. The technique was instilled in them at school and polished by society. *And required of them by circumstance*, she reflected sadly.

Hugo spotted them and Cordelia wanted to turn and hide. "I cannot decide," she said in a panic. "And here he comes to escort me down the stairs! Oh, Ruby, what shall I do?"

"Kick him hard between the legs?"

Cordelia shifted her weight as he approached. But her shoes were soft and for the indoors, and would be unlikely to have the impact she would hope for.

He smiled wolfishly as he came to within a few steps below her. His teeth shone below his whiskers and she felt like Little Red Riding Hood. The colour of her dress was not working. She felt cold.

"There are so many people here to meet you," he said. "I am sure that you will not disappoint them."

She stared at him. What had he told them? Did they think it an engagement party? Did he trust to her good breeding that she would go along with it and not make a scene? Did he hope to trap her by social propriety and convention?

He let his smile drop a little but it was replaced by a sinister frown. "What ails you?" he asked.

She tipped her head back. So, she was to act as his intended, was she? "You did not say hello, or greet me warmly, or compliment my dress, or my hair, or any such thing," she said. "I expected more."

He laughed. "Oh, Cordelia, you are a woman of the world. What need have you of silly compliments and frippery? I thought you were past all that."

Past. Not above; *past*. It was her turn to frown. "So, Hugo, do all these fine folk think that you have proposed marriage to me?"

"Yes, and that you have accepted. I did so hate to disappoint them. Still, if you want to tell them all to go home..."

"You did *not* propose; I certainly did *not* accept."

"Oh, Cordelia." He softened his voice and stepped up to the same level as her, coming in close so he could lower his voice. He started to sound as if he were a stage mesmerist. "I appreciate it's all a whirl for you, and a lot to take in. And I must apologise. I told you before that I am a rough sort of man, and unused to flattery and the finer ways of courting. I hope that you can come to love me as I am, plain, simple, unpretentious..."

She stepped to one side, seeing him with more clarity. "You just assume I will acquiesce, don't you? That I'll give it all up – the wager, Clarfields – and marry you? That it's all been a game of hard-to-get on my part, some silly diversion. Men like you can't hear the word 'no', can you?" She saw it plainly now. He would never accept no.

And maybe, she thought, he was worried that she *would* solve the case and he would have to stick to the wager. The coroner had witnessed it, after all. Front, face, impression – Hugo could not be seen as a man who broke his word.

"You are afraid I might win the wager," she said.

"That silly thing?"

"Yes. You cannot take the chance, can you? You feel you have to put pressure on me now and settle the matter."

"Marry me, Cordelia."

"And what of the wager?"

"Marry me, Cordelia! I know that you will have a happy home here."

"I will *never* marry you! You are a trickster and a sneak." She said it loudly, and noted that heads were beginning to turn. People had come for a party; she resolved that she may as well provide them with a show. It was as if something flipped inside her.

She was done with it all.

"Cordelia, Cordelia, calm yourself. Shall I send for a little drop of something to still your nerves?"

It was the way of things. It had always been the way of things. *Powerful men*, she thought, who strode through life expecting the world to be a certain way – and such was the force of their confidence that *lo!* The world *was* a certain way.

No.

"Hugo Hawke, I did not agree to marry you. And I shall not marry you!" She shouted it now. Everyone heard.

Silence settled on the gathering. Every face was turned to look. Hugo's teeth were still showing, but now in a snarl, not a smile. He had underestimated her, she knew. "We will discuss this privately."

She knew what that meant. Oh, she had plenty of experience from her first marriage. It meant being locked up until she conceded defeat.

She sucked in a deep breath.

And kneed him sharply between the legs.

The dragging effect of her skirts meant she lost some of the force but none of the surprise and every man present gasped and groaned at the sight. She stepped back and Ruby was at her side. Her maid's hand was on Cordelia's upper back and it seemed to pour strength into Cordelia like magic. Hugo lunged forward, wildly, his hands reaching out like claws to grab her wrists.

She had expected it. She retreated along the landing, staying by the wall rather than the railings and bannisters. People began to rush up the steps to keep her in view, and Hugo took two steps to follow her, before someone bellowed out, "No!"

She did not know who it was, but Hugo did stop.

"I did not agree to marry you!" she shouted again, a public declaration that could not now be in doubt.

He was puffing his cheeks in and out, and his face was becoming more red as he glared.

Finally he spoke.

"Get out of my house. Now."

CHAPTER THIRTY

It was absolutely freezing.

"What happened to summer?" Ruby complained. "How can the temperature drop so suddenly?" She burbled on, spouting an endless and meaningless litany about the weather. Cordelia didn't mind. It was something to focus on as they waited, huddled together, just past the entrance to Hugo's manor. They were standing at the edge of the public road, desperately seeking shelter from the incessant rain. They were wearing nothing but their gowns designed for indoor activities. Ruby was slightly better placed as she had not been a guest at the party, so she was wearing her more-sensible clothing, the usual mixture of modified cast-offs from Cordelia. Cordelia had nothing but her red dress, many skirts, thin gloves and a shawl that a purse-lipped matron had thrust into her hands as Cordelia had fled through the crowd and out the front door, pursued by Hugo.

He chased them both, Ruby and Cordelia, until they were clear of his land. With more foul invectives and cursing, he stood in the rain for a moment, until he grew bored. Then he turned and half-ran back into his house, shouting that all Cordelia's staff were to be ejected without delay.

"I should go back in," Ruby said. "I must gather your things."

Cordelia wanted to ask her to stay, but she knew it was sense, and she let her go.

Now she was alone.

* * *

Carriages and coaches began to pass by as guests left in a hurry. She imagined the chatter within, as she shrank back against the wall and tried to stay out of sight. She and Hugo would be the talk of the locality for many months to come. No one mourned a poor working man's death, but the public scene was quite the scandal! At least she did not live here, and though the gossip would follow her home, she did not feel as affected as she knew that Hugo would. It would strike him deeply.

Her feet were cold and she felt as if she were slowly sinking into the mud. The wall offered slight protection and she pressed against it. Above her, a tree dropped slow, fat balls of rain onto her bare head.

She would never be allowed to be a guest here again.

And no doubt she would have fewer invitations to go visiting elsewhere, too, once word spread of her shenanigans.

A succession of three carriages rumbled past, their wheels sticking in the mud and the horses prancing with their hooves high and their eyes wild and rolling. But the third slowed to a stop at the entrance, and she pressed even harder against the stone.

Oh! It was her own travelling chariot; the bulk of the thing was so different to the light little carriages that people had used to come to the party. Atop the driver's seat was the spiky form of Stanley, recognisable even under his splay-shouldered oilskin cape. He was peering about him as if he had been told roughly where to find her.

She went forward. "Here!"

"My lady!" He jumped down into the dark wet mud, and helped her into the carriage. She tried to keep her filthy skirts clear of the upholstery but it was no use and she shuddered to see the brown trail she had left. One lantern was lit within, and it was enough; even the sight of it warmed her. "I will draw to the side," he said, "and we will await the others."

"Where are they?"

"They are coming," he said. He smiled, and in the darkness he met her eyes, and she realised that in the excitement, his stammer had receded. She did not mention it. She thanked him, and let him close the door upon her.

* * *

She wrapped herself up well in the furs and blankets of the coach, and settled back, worrying about her staff and her possessions. She wanted Stanley to come in and talk to her, keep her company, but he had his place and it was outside in the driving rain as he, too, waited anxiously.

The first to appear was Geoffrey. She heard his voice, talking to Stanley in a low gruff way. Then the coach rocked and she heard the boxes on the back being opened and closed. There was another slam, and then silence.

She poked her head out of the window, but could see nothing in the blackness. "Are you all right up there?"

Only Stanley answered. "Yes, my lady."

Then Ruby and Mrs Unsworth appeared and there was more activity as things were tied to the roof and the back. A chest of clothes was shoved into the main carriage, and Ruby and Mrs Unsworth climbed in after it, their legs shoved up awkwardly against the chest which took up most of the floor-space. Ruby had brought a hot brick wrapped well in old, thin woollen fabric, and Cordelia clung to it.

The door opened again, as soon as it had closed. Geoffrey stood there, large in his layers, a dark shadow with the rain pouring off his hat. "Are we all fit to go?" he asked.

Cordelia nodded wearily. "I believe so. It is the journey of many hours to get home; they will be rather surprised, don't you think?" *Surprised at everything,* she thought sadly. *Particularly surprised at the news we are to leave. Though I suppose most of them will be expecting this. I cannot imagine that the trusteeship was any kind of secret to the staff.*

She could not see Geoffrey's expression clearly but his

face screwed up. Ruby leaned forward and blocked most of the light from the lantern. Now Cordelia could hardly see anything.

"But we are not going home, my lady," Geoffrey said.

"What do you mean? Are the horses unwell? I think Hugo will have a fit all over again if we stayed here."

"We are not staying here," Geoffrey said brusquely. "I have got us rooms at the inn. Let's go."

He slammed the door and the coach shifted on its springs as he climbed up. Ruby sat back, smiling smugly. Even Mrs Unsworth's face was a little softer.

"It's a bad idea," Cordelia said. "We may as well press on now, and be home by first light. Why bother staying over, just to delay the start before we head home?"

"As Geoffrey says, my lady, we're not going home," Ruby said. "Not tonight and not tomorrow, neither."

Mrs Unsworth spoke unexpectedly. "Been there, done that, eh, my lady?"

"I'm sorry?"

"You done that before. Letting the man call the shots. You're different now. You don't let 'em do that, and good luck to you, and all."

"What happened before?" Ruby asked.

Both Cordelia and Mrs Unsworth turned to look at her. Neither was going to speak. Ruby swallowed and dropped her gaze.

Cordelia turned back to the task in hand. "I do not see the value in staying. I don't wish to taunt the man. It is all over."

"You ain't staying for that man. You are staying for the other," Mrs Unsworth said. "Fool's errand though it is. But you may as well see it through. For him. And for us, and Clarfields, I reckon."

Ruby nodded. "You have business to conclude here, my lady."

"I do." *Oh goodness, oh no.* Cordelia pulled the furs around her as the carriage lurched forward, its progress made jerky by the bad ruts that were emerging in the mud. She felt warmed now, from the inside, and it wasn't just the effect of the blankets.

But she was also nervous. For now she had to live up to her servants' faith in her.

CHAPTER THIRTY-ONE

The journey through the black countryside was short, but slow. Stanley walked ahead with a lantern, slipping and sliding in the mud, while Geoffrey urged the horses on at a steady and careful pace. With no moon and no stars, the road was treacherous in its darkness. Cordelia held the curtain back from the window in the door, peeping out until the first sight of a yellow light made her smile.

The lights grew more frequent; now they were entering the outskirts of the small town. The meaner cottages had but one candle, or were lit only by a fire. Some still used rank and smelly rush-lights, due to the proximity to the reed beds of the fens. The larger dwellings had more abundant lanterns and lamps.

Finally they came onto the main street, and the inn was lit like a beacon to attract all weary travellers. Geoffrey drove the carriage around to the yard, through the wide arch and into a well-lit and active space. The staff of the inn were ready for coaches at any time of the day or night. They also had a regular stage and mail timetable, and were well versed in coping with people of all stations in life.

Ruby and Cordelia were swept into the inn by a tall, stately woman while Mrs Unsworth, Stanley and Geoffrey set about their various tasks; Stanley and Geoffrey to the horses and thence to the taproom, while Mrs Unsworth directed the unloading of the essential luggage.

Geoffrey had done his work well. Cordelia found that he had engaged a small suite of rooms to house them all, and she was glad that they were all going to be together and not scattered across the inn. There was a small room for Geoffrey and Stanley, a truckle bed erected in a day room for Mrs Unsworth, and a slightly larger room for Cordelia with another truckle bed in there, tucked half behind a curtain in an alcove, for Ruby. It wasn't exactly ideal in the normal scheme of things. It ought to have been scandalous. But these were no longer normal times.

The fire was well-lit. A maid bobbed and curtseyed and fussed until Cordelia assured her that all was well, and paid her to go away. Then they set about stripping out of their wet gowns. Mrs Unsworth soon lumbered in with fresh clothing for all, and Cordelia was curled before the fire with a warm brew in her hands by the time Geoffrey and Stanley came up. They stood awkwardly by the door.

"Come in," she said, waving her hands.

Geoffrey did so, but Stanley was paralysed by impropriety and stayed where he was.

"Have you ladies all eaten?" Geoffrey asked. "I can recommend the broth. Very hearty."

"I am not sure I can face food yet," Cordelia said.

She then caught sight of Mrs Unsworth's face. Her expression of misery was mirrored on Ruby's. Cordelia smiled. "However, I think these two should go and eat; I can take care of myself."

"You insult me to say that," Ruby said tartly as she got to her feet.

"I'm sorry, Ruby. I mean to say, *I should be lost without you*. Now, go, the pair of you. Geoffrey, Stanley; do not feel obliged to attend on me. Go back to the taproom. Drink, relax, don't lose too much at cards or dice or whatever it is you may play there."

"Push-penny," Geoffrey said, "And I am the master at it."

"Go forth, then, and dominate," she said.

Stanley was reluctant to go back down. *He would be happier with a quiet space and a book,* she thought, but Geoffrey grabbed him and steered him back onto the landing.

As soon as she was alone, she felt energy beginning to seep back into her bones. She watched the fire for a while, poking sticks onto it from time to time. There was a coal scuttle nearby and she threw some coals onto the flames, damping it down to a solid, steady heat. She thought briefly about where the coal was delivered from, but realised she was trying to distract herself from the real business to which she had to attend.

She was growing hungry, now. It was around ten o'clock and she could hear laughter and occasional distant shouts from elsewhere. She was gripped by the desire to prowl and explore. This was where Mrs Hurrell had been held; she decided, on a whim, to sally forth and discover the room for herself.

She pulled a grey shawl around her shoulders, and did not pay attention to her still-damp and now-frizzing hair.

She did not want to terrify any maids who would not be expecting a well-bred lady to be abroad in the corridors; better it be that she seem to be a more middling sort. She spotted a woman in black who was running with a tray of food, and Cordelia stopped her to ask where Mrs Hurrell had been kept.

The maid looked alarmed. "Why do you want to know?" she demanded.

Why, indeed? Cordelia rounded her shoulders a little and hoped she didn't look too haughty. She said, "I bet a lot of folks have been pestering you, wanting to see the woman."

"Not really. Everyone's seen her before anyway. Are you a guest here…?"

"Yes, yes, I am. Sorry for keeping you from your work."

As the maid turned to go, Cordelia said, "Oh, and the room?"

Rolling her eyes, the maid nodded down the hallway. "At the end. It's a store room usually. No windows, see?"

Cordelia waited until the maid was out of sight, and then went along the corridor. The carpet ran out and became bare floorboards as she turned a corner, and the lamps along here were sparse. The few lamps there were seemed to give out a light that was almost beige. She spotted the correct door instantly; it had two heavy bolts on it, at the top and at the bottom.

She would not have been able to explain why she felt so compelled to see the room. Perhaps she was just another gawper like those at a hanging, delighting to witness another's dreadful fate.

But then, she reminded herself, Mrs Hurrell had escaped the noose.

Cordelia reached the door. All was quiet. There was a wooden chair by the door, presumably for a constable or watchman to use. Only the top bolt was shot home, so she jumped up onto the chair, holding her skirts with one hand and steadying herself against the wall with the other. It was a quick and simple task to drag the bolt back; its recent frequent use had kept it supple.

And then she was able to swing the door open, and look in.

Nothing. There was simply nothing unremarkable about the room. It was dark and unlit, but by the filtering light of the lanterns in the corridor, she could see it was small and had a narrow bed along one side. That was all. The maid had been wrong; there was a small skylight, narrow and high. For some reason, Cordelia found herself relieved to see that. Perhaps she couldn't quite bear the thought of anyone being kept in total darkness from day to day.

So, the coroner and the sheriff were done with the case, were they? It was to be ascribed to a "wandering vagrant" and done with it.

No. He was killed deliberately, she was sure of it. Someone came to that house, sent Mrs Hurrell away with a note, and knocked him out.

Cordelia stood bolt upright then and her heart thudded in surprise as a fresh idea struck her.

If the note did exist, had it really been part of it, all along?

Or was it an unrelated event that she had ascribed a meaning to – a meaning that it did not have?

Was the killer, in fact, seeking Mrs Hurrell all along?

CHAPTER THIRTY-TWO

The next day began slowly, and Cordelia kept to her rooms while her servants went about their tasks. She sent Stanley and Mrs Unsworth out to gather gossip from their respective social groups, and Geoffrey lingered in the stables, seeing to the coach and talking to travellers. She set Ruby to attend to a particular objective, and the maid went off to fulfil that willingly.

Cordelia flicked through her notebook, stared at the fire, drank an awful lot of tea, and thought about the crime.

She was sure that she was close.

Always, she asked herself, *who benefits?*

* * *

"At last!" Ruby cried as she burst into the room where

Cordelia still sat. "I am sorry I took so long."

"It is no matter – you are here, now. Sit, take a drink."

Ruby thrust the bundle of letters at Cordelia. "You see," she said, "now aren't you grateful that I got to know those footmen so well?"

"Foot*men?*"

"Eggs, baskets, you know," Ruby said airily. "But they were easily persuaded to keep your correspondence hidden from Hugo and pass it on to me."

"Marvellous."

Cordelia riffled through the letters that had been addressed to her care of the manor house. There was one advantage to being a lady writer, failed or not; her agent and others were most amenable to playing along with her whims and demands. After all, they were not the ones who were out of pocket with her ventures.

Ruby sat quietly while Cordelia read through the notes. Most were of no use. They started with three paragraphs of social platitudes, then remarked that no information could be found, and followed that up with a further four paragraphs of meaningless society gossip.

But there were a few gems in amongst it all. She sat back.

"You are smiling, my lady…" Ruby said, not able to hide her own grin of curiosity. "Do tell."

"It mostly concerns our mysterious Mrs Hurrell," Cordelia said. "A woman with a past."

"The most interesting sort of woman," Ruby said.

"Indeed. Though I would counsel you to avoid Mrs Hurrell's particular way of becoming interesting; you know, I think, that she ran a house of ill-repute in London?"

"I did. I remember we thought no more of it."

"But there is more," Cordelia said. "This confirms it. She served a sentence of several months' imprisonment for it. Hard labour, no less. And then she came here, to start afresh."

"Commendable."

It was similar to the newspaper article she had read that had been hidden in the sideboard. A different woman; the same outcome. Crime, then punishment.

"The past has a horrid way of catching up with us," Cordelia said sadly. She shook herself free of that, and ploughed on. "Anyway. So, Mrs Hurrell came here. And that had got me to thinking. Why here, do you think?"

"I don't know. Why anywhere?"

"I think that I know," Cordelia said. "Ewatt Carter-Hall was one of her many clients in London. He is a man with appetites, and he made no secret of that to me. She had an especial talent for finding innocent girls who had recently arrived in the city seeking their fortune. Alas, they found something quite the opposite. And it is suggested that she came here with a small sum of money that Ewatt gave her to start her lodging house. And there is more. Who owns that house?"

"I am guessing that it is not Mrs Hurrell…"

"Indeed not. Mr Carter-Hall owns it, as Mrs Kale told us."

Ruby chewed her lip reflectively. "So they *are* linked."

"They are, in more ways than I had thought."

Both lapsed into silence for a while. From time to time, Ruby made a suggestion – "Mrs Hurrell did it" or "Mr Carter-Hall and his wife did it" or even "could it have been a passing vagrant and we are but fools?"

Cordelia dismissed it all, saying, "We must find the *why* and from there we find the *who.*"

The meditation was broken by the arrival of Stanley. He stammered out the information he had heard in the servants' halls around the town.

"Mrs Hurrell had been targeted before," he said. "By a burglar, I mean."

"What happened?"

"N-nothing, my lady. She surprised him and he ran off."

"He?"

"An unknown man. Skinny, rough-voiced, and very tall."

Cordelia tapped her fingers on her now-empty cup. "So. There is something in Mrs Hurrell's possession that another wants."

"Was it only a burglary gone wrong?" Ruby asked. She sounded almost disappointed.

"We saw nothing in her house. Perhaps the burglar was successful. However, I rather think that the burglary was but a part of the whole."

"And what of the doctor?" Ruby said. "Is he no longer a suspect? Was that all a dead-end?"

Cordelia smiled. "I suspect him of a few things," she said. "Let us unravel this all. There is to be a ball tomorrow night, in Cambridge, is there not?"

Stanley and Ruby looked at one another and shrugged.

"Well, there is," Cordelia went on. "It is marking the end of the summer, but it will be a more impressive thing than Hugo's little gathering. Many will be returning to London for the opening of Parliament; others will be heading for the hunting, as Hugo will. Ruby, fetch my writing desk and open it on that table there. Stanley, wait one moment; I have another task for you. A message will need delivering to Mr Carter-Hall. Oh, and I wish to speak to Mrs Unsworth too. She needs to go into town for me."

She strode to her portable writing desk and bent to her task. Mrs Unsworth announced her presence by heavy breathing as she stood at the door. Eventually Cordelia was ready. She pressed a list of items into Mrs Unsworth's hand. "You are to go shopping," she told her. "And take Ruby, for I value her good taste."

Then she turned to Stanley. "This note, you must put directly into Ewatt Carter-Hall's hand. Not his post box, not onto the tray in his hall, not into the hand of the housekeeper or a steward or a butler. The man himself. Do you understand?"

"Y-yes my lady."

"Good."

There was a moment of stillness.

"Go on, be about it!" she said, and ushered them all from the room.

Now, she waited.

She seemed to be doing quite a lot of that recently. But it was a waiting that was filled with potential.

CHAPTER THIRTY-THREE

Sir William Elkesley's Cambridge residence was on a grand scale. Cordelia liked to think of herself as above being impressed by worldly show and extravagance, but it would be a hard heart indeed that was not amazed by the vast rooms, high ceilings, crowded paintings in deep gilt frames, and every manner of sculpture and decoration throughout.

The butler greeted them impassively and nodded.

Cordelia's mouth was dry.

The announcement was made. "Ewatt Carter-Hall and–" There was just a slight pause. "–and Cordelia, Lady Cornbrook."

Heads turned. Perhaps not everyone knew of the scandal that had led to her being expelled from Hugo Hawke's manor, but certainly enough people *did* know that a ripple of low conversation spread in expanding circles from knots of people who were standing around.

Ewatt's hand was steady. He led her forwards and bent to whisper in her ear. "Fear not, dear Cordelia. As your escort, I shall aid you to navigate these choppy waters. Your bravery astounds me; I am delighted to be prevailed upon to help you brazen this out."

"Thank you so much," she murmured back to him.

Indeed, he had sent a reply to her message by instant return; nothing would give him greater pleasure, he had said, than to accompany her to this grand ball. Obtaining invitations to it would be simple for a man such as himself.

And everyone from the great and the good would be present, she knew. And so, the trap was set. She stood tall and cast her eye about. Many people reddened and looked away hastily. A few met her gaze with a steady look, unfazed by her actions. One or two winked, and she felt a few fellow sympathisers lend her strength in their nods and slight smiles.

There was the coroner, of course, and his short, mousey wife.

"Is the sheriff here, do you know?" she asked Ewatt.

"No idea," he answered brusquely. "I think he favours Huntingdonshire, to be truthful. We are just a little too …

rural, perhaps, for his tastes."

She craned her neck. She hoped that Geoffrey had done his work and got the constables in place. She had sent him to seek out the watch committee though they seemed far more interested in trying to make the university contribute to the payment of watchmen. Stanley had had his tasks, too; he assured her that he had passed messages on to the coroner and the sheriff. But neither had sent any reply to her.

There was Doctor Donald Arnall and his wife. He was not looking her way, and for that she was glad. Knowing what she knew about him now made her uncomfortable. She was not sure what to do with that knowledge.

A tug on her arm reminded her that the initial source for that knowledge, Ewatt himself, was waiting.

She smiled at him. He had followed her gaze. "I am amazed that man is here so blatantly," he muttered.

Cordelia had sent an entreaty to Hetty, via Ruby. She was not sure what had had the most persuasive effect; her letter or Ruby herself. She was happy to see it had worked, and that Hetty had brought her husband along.

Her letter had contained the words, "Some revelations

may be painful but I can assure you that it is all in the name of justice." Perhaps that had done the trick.

"My dear, are you quite all right?" Ewatt said.

"I am sorry. Do forgive me." Cordelia had been standing still and taking it all in, running through events in her mind. "Please. Shall we mingle?"

"Allow me." He led her into the throng of people, and they began to smile and chat with anyone who would not melt away in embarrassment.

* * *

She was waiting for her moment. Her heart had been thudding in her chest for so long now that she wondered how much more it could take. Perhaps she should have just written her suspicions out to the sheriff; but then, she reminded herself, she would not see justice done.

No, her revelations had to be made in public. The coroner must know of it, and Clarfields would be saved. All the parties involved must be present.

Almost all the parties involved.

She could see no way to bring Mrs Hurrell from

London to witness this, though the events concerned her most of all.

Still, the other principle players were present. And as she still lacked some essential proof – beyond her own gut feelings – she needed to make the revelations in front of the guilty party and hope that their reactions would seal their fate.

Now she needed to orchestrate them all together, and her palms were slippery with sweat in her fine white gloves.

She was enclosed by people. The music from the quartet in an adjoining room seemed to grow louder and louder. The more she concentrated, the more overwhelmed she began to feel. A woman's braying laugh scored fingernails through her mind. A man turned, his eyes huge, his mouth wet and his lips hanging loosely. She almost swooned, such was the intensity.

Ewatt's hand gripped her upper arm, and she staggered.

"I have you," he said.

"Thank you."

"Do you need to sit? Here – well, here is the doctor. He may as well be of some use."

And there he was, the lean, lithe Doctor Arnall, approaching with his wife at his side. She peered at Cordelia with curiosity, and not a little apprehension.

It was falling into place. Cordelia dragged a deep breath into her lungs and straightened up. She stared past Doctor Arnall. "Is that the sheriff?"

At hearing his title, the whiskered man turned his head in her direction. He was old but hale, a hearty man who had ridden hard in his youth and retained his fitness even in his advancing years. His hearing, too, was as undimmed as his sight, and his perception that something was potentially amiss.

He approached the little group.

Now was the moment.

Now was the time.

Cordelia put her own hand over Ewatt's where it rested on her upper arm. And she held on.

"Sheriff," she said. "May I present to you the murderer of Thomas Bains."

CHAPTER THIRTY-FOUR

She was expecting a sudden hush.

What she got was laughter.

It was stilted at first, nervous, hesitant.

Then the sheriff began to laugh, and others followed suit.

Cordelia wanted to curl up and cry.

But then she noticed that in spite of the laughter, people were curious. They were gathering around. Ewatt's hand on her arm was digging in, now, almost to the point of discomfort. His knuckles were white. That was her proof. This was exactly the moment she had been working towards, she told herself.

She inclined her head towards Ewatt, and said, "How goes your banking business, Ewatt?"

The laughter faded as people strove to hear what was

being said. The sudden change of direction grabbed everyone's attention.

"It rumbles along quite nicely," he said. There was a flat, dangerous light in his eyes. He did not want to speak of it.

"Does it?" she said. "You would not be the first owner of a small local bank to raise loans in London against your supposed stock – loans that you know can never be repaid."

"What nonsense," Ewatt said. "You know nothing of the financial world."

"The world of fake money, of false investments, of illusory projects? I know enough. You had to maintain a face so that your investors would not get edgy and pull out. But your bank was nothing more than a name on a door, Ewatt, and still you raised money, planning to flee abroad with it."

"You know *nothing*," he repeated.

"I know enough to know that you were in deep financial trouble," she said. "There were signs. You never called the doctor to your sick children."

His face paled. "Do not accuse me of neglect, madam! How dare you throw our private grief into such a foul slander."

"Oh, I don't think that you failed to call the doctor because of lack of funds to pay him. For I know that the doctor – notwithstanding some foolish decisions he has made in the past – the doctor is a good man and would not suffer to see a child die if he could in any wise prevent it, money or not. No, you let your babes die so that you could collect on the insurance."

There was a collective gasp.

"Madam! I–"

"No," she said, cutting him off. "It is a common practise, I understand, amongst the lower orders. My maid reminded me of that. There are death clubs and burial clubs, where money is put aside for the costs of a funeral. But in your case, Ewatt, you let the children wither and fade rather than even try to save them! You had utterly divorced yourself, in your mind, from family life. You thought only of your plans to escape. No wonder your wife flirts with madness and despair."

"This is insanity!" he spluttered. "And you have no evidence."

"Only what I saw with my own eyes," she said. "But I

would urge that auditors go to your bank and see for themselves. For it is the sad decline of your fortunes that has put everything else into motion."

Ewatt puffed out his cheeks and thought furiously, his emotions chasing over his red face. "Well – well," he said. "Though my bank's dealings do rise and sometimes fall, as do all businesses, yet I cannot see how you can possibly link that to anything else, least of all the death of some man."

"It is very much linked," she said. "You owned the house that Mrs Hurrell rented, and she sub-let that back room. You wanted to put her rent up. Yet you did not. You *could* not."

"Of course I could. It is a balance," he said, trying to sound calm and reasonable once more. "If I raise my rents too high, my tenants will leave. So…"

"No," she said, stopping him. "She had information about you, Ewatt, and she threatened to expose you. Her rent was low, and it was to remain so, because you could not risk raising it! And more than that. You wanted to get that information back. So you sent a man to rob her, but he was surprised in the execution of it. So you went yourself, did you not?"

"What utter rot."

The sheriff had been listening and now he spoke. "But it was a young man who was killed," he said. "I fail to see the connection with rents and robberies."

"Thomas Bains rented the back room," Cordelia said. "And though he was a loud sort of man, he was also, in his own strange way, a good one. A man's actions speak louder than words, do they not? However loud one's words might be. I heard so many examples of *things* that Thomas had done – he gave his coat to a beggar, he helped others in small ways – that I got a sense of him being, in his own way, a moral being."

Everyone was shaking their heads, unconvinced. Cordelia stormed on with her explanation. "No, it is true. And it was Thomas who fitted the post box to Ewatt's house, and Thomas who began to learn of the bank's problems and his need for secrecy in this matter."

"So why did Thomas not make this public?" the sheriff asked. He still didn't look as if he believed a word of it.

"He tried." Cordelia pointed through the crowd around her, and her object was the doctor. "He sought out the one man in the town that he thought he could trust.

The one person who had a social standing, but who was not part of the corrupt ring of players. Doctor Donald Arnall."

The doctor shook his head. "He did not."

"He did," said Hetty, at his shoulder. "He came ... and you sent him away." Her face was very pale. "And why did you do that, Don?"

"He ... I ... it was unconnected," he stammered.

"No," Cordelia said sadly. "I am sorry to have to do this, and I will be succinct if I may. Due to certain events in your past, doctor, you had reason to think that Thomas had come to try to blackmail you. He was not talking directly, I imagine, and nor did you. It is our way, is it not, to edge around the truth and never say a direct thing if it is a disagreeable thing? And I know that I am doing the same thing now; alluding most vaguely to hidden matters. But it is not my revelation to make. Suffice it to say that you believed Thomas was talking to you about your past mistakes ... and he was not."

The doctor's face crumpled and he grabbed Hetty, dragging her close to his side. "Oh no."

"Can it be true?" the sheriff demanded.

"What she says – about me, and Thomas. Yes. It is true. I sent him away. I misunderstood. Oh, had I listened! I am a fool. He might be yet alive."

Indeed he might, Cordelia thought, but saw no reason to fuel his misery. Kindly, she said, "There were other things at play. Indeed, when Ewatt went to Mrs Hurrell's that fateful morning, he did not, I believe, intend to kill. He sent a note to get Mrs Hurrell out of the house. All he wanted was what he believed that she kept in her sideboard. She had told him she had evidence – of his bank's collapse, of his involvement in scandals in London, all manner of things. They knew one another in London. He helped her to set up a new home here, and that was foolish of him. He had more to lose than her, you see. And he realised he could not risk it when she began to threaten to expose him." *And why didn't she? The papers were no evidence, Cordelia thought. She could not do more than make an accusation that all would laugh off.*

But I am a gentlewoman, and people must listen.

She continued. "So he went to retrieve this evidence. He thought that Thomas was working at the manor, as usual."

"But he wasn't," the doctor breathed.

"No; once again he had argued with Ralph Goody over the theft of vegetables and meat. Ralph runs a profitable side-line in selling pilfered goods. So Thomas was out of work, and lying on his bed in the back room when Ewatt entered."

Ewatt had let go of her arm and he started to back away. Suddenly there were two constables at his back. These were town watchmen, and used to using their brawn in pub fights and street altercations. Ewatt was stuck.

Cordelia made brief eye contact with the sheriff and he nodded. She continued. "Thomas had decided to confront Ewatt about his business. He knew that once Ewatt had siphoned off as much money as he could, by the matter of raising loans against his non-existent capital and his fake stocks, he was going to disappear. It would not be the first time a regional bank had done this. He was planning to go abroad – I know this from conversations with the post master and also his wife. But Thomas could not let that happen. He could not keep his mouth shut. He'd heard the threats and arguments between Mrs Hurrell and Ewatt, and he knew Ewatt was up to no good. The doctor had spurned him. So it was left to Thomas, that rash impulsive man, in the spur of the moment, to come into Mrs Hurrell's room and confront Ewatt."

By now, everyone was hanging on her every word. She paused and dropped her voice.

"The result was sadly inevitable. An argument, possibly a scuffle; Ewatt could not let Thomas go, and Thomas was too impulsive to stop, think and walk away. What then happened, only Ewatt can tell us. But certainly a punch was thrown, a left-handed blow, and Thomas hit his head, and died."

She stopped. That was it; all her conjecture and all her suppositions, laid out for the sheriff to assess. Some of it had taken leaps of imagination. Some of it was guesswork. She looked to her side.

And her intuition was rewarded.

Ewatt was white in the face, and his eyes bulged. Even as he began to protest, saying, "No, no, arrest this mad woman for slander!" the constables were at either side of him. He began to flail his arms, and they restrained him, pulling his arms back to snap some large, heavy cuffs on his wrists.

"An innocent man would not fight," the sheriff

remarked drily, stepping up close to Ewatt and peering at him. "Certainly I am interested, in the first instance, to examine your banking affairs a little more closely."

"You cannot! I forbid it!" Ewatt said. "I am innocent, innocent, caught in these lies by an unhinged woman!"

"All the women you deal with seem to end up unhinged," Cordelia said. "Mrs Hurrell was right to flee when she could."

"You–"

His curses and blasphemy were loud and violent, and even the sheriff winced. He nodded at his constables who began to haul Ewatt away, still protesting.

"My lady," he said, turning back to Cordelia. "I cannot say what will come of this. You have given us much to ponder on, and I am afraid that man does not help his case with his reaction. And now I see you are without an escort. Do allow me." He offered his arm, and she accepted, with relief flooding through her like a wave.

"Thank you," she said.

They moved off, and the crowd followed. From between the heads, she saw the coroner, John Barron.

He smiled.

Suddenly, everyone wanted to talk to Cordelia again. She was a part of things once more.

And Clarfields was hers.

CHAPTER THIRTY-FIVE

"Another afternoon visit; another dramatic reconstruction of the events that occurred at Wallerton Manor," Cordelia said as Ruby helped her attend to her dress.

"You love it, my lady," Ruby said cheekily. "There's Mrs Collins out there, and the reverend's wife also. You cannot wait to scandalise them with your recount."

"I? Oh, Ruby, all I wanted was for justice to prevail."

"*Your* justice," Ruby said. "And to keep this place yours. Clarfields. There, now. Your hair is just right. Oh, I should tell you that Geoffrey has argued with Mr Fry *again*."

Would the feud between the butler and the coachman never end? Cordelia rolled her eyes to heaven and sighed. "And Mrs Unsworth? She seemed a little happier to be back in her own kitchen when I went to talk about this week's menu."

"Mrs Unsworth? Who can say what goes on in that old stick's heart and mind. I, for one, don't care to find out."

"You ought to be kinder to her," Cordelia said.

"Why?"

But Cordelia could not explain. It was not her story to tell. She straightened her skirts and threw back her head, and sallied out to meet another group of callers.

* * *

In truth, everything had felt ever so slightly different since they had returned home. Cordelia had slept like a baby in the carriage, and barely remembered being helped into bed. The servants slipped back into their dedicated duties, but everything was shifted one step to the right, or set on a diagonal. Her previous lady's maid had but briefly returned from her holiday. She had packed her things, muttered something about a man, and departed. So Ruby stepped into the position on a permanent basis.

Geoffrey and Stanley melted back into the coach house and she barely saw them. Mrs Unsworth was once more queen of her own kitchens and the respite the maids of the house had enjoyed was now broken. But her surly manner remained. Cordelia could not bring herself to correct it.

And scandal had followed, as scandal does, but with the accolades and praise of the sheriff and the press to counteract her unwomanly doings, it all seemed to even out. Some snooty types would not speak to her. She was glad of it. Those that were worth anything, still came to see her.

"My lady? My lady? Mrs Collins, ring the bell—"

"No, no, I am sorry. I was far away." Cordelia blinked and shook herself, and felt herself redden slightly. She hoped she had not actually fallen asleep but the reverend's wife's homilies had an opiate effect on a person.

The reverend's wife, Lottie Melshaw, patted her hand. "We were asking about the murderer's poor mad wife."

"Ah." In truth, Cordelia thought that Freda was not mad at all. Perhaps silly, perhaps easily influenced, certainly too focused on material things and the help she could find in a bottle of laudanum. "The children were taken by the doctor and his wife, and I cannot think of a better pair to bring up healthy offspring. As for Freda herself … there was talk of holding her to account but under the law, no way forward could be seen. And she solved the problem herself by running away with a passing businessman. I say businessman; he was a young man with a certain inherited fortune who was off to the Americas to make something of himself. She always wanted to travel. So she has not been pursued."

"She should be tried for her neglect of her children," Mrs Collins said stoutly.

"She will, at the gates of heaven," Mrs Melshaw said, and Cordelia gave her a wide and grateful smile. For all Freda's faults, Cordelia blamed much of it on her husband.

It was strange how a man could turn his wife into a criminal, she thought, and bile rose into her mouth as the memories came back. She must have blanched, for Mrs Melshaw reached forward to pat her hand once more. Her touch was warm and comforting.

"You've had such a trying time, dear. I imagine you'll be quite content to stay at home for the rest of your life!"

How perfectly dreadful. The memories receded. Cordelia sat up defiantly. "Oh no," she said. "In a few months' time I shall be heading north to see my aunt, Maude Stanbury."

"North?" both matriarchs gasped in horror.

"Far north," Cordelia said, enjoying their reaction immensely. "Yorkshire. But do not worry. My aunt lives the quiet life of an elderly spinster, in a beautiful rural area, I am told. It is all rolling moors and babbling brooks."

"In November?" Mrs Collins asked.

"Well, perhaps they are *cold* rolling moors and iced-over brooks. But what could possibly be more relaxing than a few weeks in a large country house on the moors…"

Thanks for reading! I'm an independent author. If you have the time, please do leave a review on Amazon. It makes a very real difference to an author's livelihood. Do note this book has been written in British English, which is just like American English but we like to use more vowels.

For news of future releases, why not sign up to my spam-free newsletter? Click here:

http://issybrooke.com/newsletter/

Look out for more adventures involving Cordelia and her retinue – coming throughout 2016.

Also available: contemporary light cozy mysteries set in Lincolnshire. The Some Very English Murders series is available here:

http://www.amazon.com/gp/product/B019U21S7C

Turn the page for my Historical Notes.

Historical Note

I have striven to be as historically accurate as possible. But I am fallible. I welcome feedback - if I've messed up, please do email me on issy@issybrooke.com or join in the discussion on my website here:

http://www.issybrooke.com. I will amend future editions.

I would ask that you point me in the direction of your sources for any corrections. The interesting thing about history is that we all tend to come at it through the lens of modern cultural interpretations. But you can't trust what you see on television; often it's a dumbed-down version that we are fed, and take as "true."

Some of the books that I have consulted are:

How To Be A Victorian by Ruth Goodman

Liberty's Dawn: A People's History of the Industrial Revolution

Children of the Mill by David Hanson

The Victorian City by Judith Flanders

WhatThe Victorians Did For Us by Adam Hart-Davis

A Very British Murder by Lucy Worsley

The Great British Bobby by Clive Emsley

The Victorian Kitchen by Jennifer Davies

The Victorian Kitchen Garden Companion by Harry Dodson

Crime and Criminals of Victorian England by Adrian Gray

Tales of a Victorian Detective by Jerome Caminada - a most excellent primary source and available cheaply on kindle

I chose 1845 because it was the very cusp of change in that century. The railways were expanding and this made travel easier but people were still using coaches and carriages. The Penny Post had just come in; the first commercial electric telegraph had begun in 1837 (and for a wonderfully gripping true tale of crime and telegraphy, read The Peculiar Case of the Electric Constable by Carol Baxter).

Regarding the system of policing at that time, again it was a time of flux. Many counties had started their own new police forces, following the lead of the Metropolitan Police in London, but some areas were resistant, especially where they feared that taxes would be raised to pay for the new constabularies. I deliberately set this book in Cambridgeshire, which in 1845 did not have its own county police force – yet. That arrived in 1851.

Cordelia is a lady but not a Lady. Ah, the details of English etiquette. She is never referred to as Lady Cordelia Cornbrook - that would mark her as one of the nobility - a lady with her own title. But as she is the wife (or, rather, widow) of a knight, Sir Cornbrook, she is called Cordelia, Lady Cornbrook or simply Lady Cornbrook, and The Dowager Lady Cornbrook. She is gentility but not nobility. Die-hard history buffs will know I've taken some liberties with Cordelia's behaviour and her interaction with her staff. Still, the fact she has money and status does give her a little leeway with regards to social conventions. There were always rebels. Interested parties should consult Debretts online.

The system of inheritance is a complex and tangled one, and things got worse for women after The Dower Act of 1834. Women tended not to inherit property.

Can you climb a six-foot wall while wearing a corset and crin-au-lin (the early incarnation of the crinoline, the large steel cages which became fashionable after 1856)? I think so. Tight-lacing was discouraged by doctors, and anyway, if you've worn such a garment all your life, you get used to moving in it. The problem would be the raising of the arms. Do check out Ruth Goodman's book, How To Be A Victorian, for detailed analysis of the effects of a woman's clothing on her everyday life. You'll be surprised - I was.

Thanks for reading!

Issy

Made in the USA
Las Vegas, NV
28 December 2021